10663723

Miracles & Wonders

Cover art by Michael S. True

Back cover photo by Edgar Sierra

I wish to dedicate this book to the krewe that makes up the Maple Leaf
Poetry Readings, (a historic weekly gathering held almost every Sunday at
the Maple Leaf Bar in New Orleans, LA). I have come to find so many
friends and fellow lovers of the written word, as well as music and art,
sharing their collective creativity in the back patio of this venerable
establishment. I would especially like to express my gratitude to those from
within this group who have inspired and supported me over the years in my
own literary journey.

Michael S. True

Published by Portals Press
www.portalspress.com

ISBN 978-0-9970666-5-4

Miracles & Wonders

5 Short Fictions

Michael S. True

Contents

Miracles

Part 1

Richard Bowman, M.D., sat comfortably in the leather upholstered driver's seat of his sky blue Jaguar XE as he navigated the familiar patchwork of misty green pastures, the yellow-brown stubble of recently harvested cornfields, and the thick wooded swaths of blazing autumn color that bordered Blue River State Park. His eyes were focused on the winding rural road that would take him the twenty-seven point five miles to the Lincoln County Mental Health Facility. He savored the weekly ride. It allowed him time to clear his mind of the day-to-day business of his medical practice back in Winfield.

Dr. Bowman pushed in a CD and listened to his favorite Paul Simon tune, "Diamonds on Her Shoes," as his thoughts turned to a weathered old man, a patient he had seen less than a half dozen times prior his placement at the secluded hospital. He could easily recall the image of the thin, unresponsive recluse that had been brought into his office by one of the county sheriff's deputies. Unable to determine the exact nature of his mental state at the time he had conferred with his colleagues at LCMHF. They had advised that a seventy-two hour hold was in order.

His patient had remained at the state-run residential facility ever since that rainy spring morning back in April. There were no apparent living relatives. A half-dozen months had already slipped past. Perhaps he would be more talkative today. Perhaps he was considering the nursing home placement that had been offered as an alternative to the lock-down in which he now resided. Maybe he finally wanted to go home.

"No more miracles. No more miracles. No more miracles," the disoriented man had repeated incessantly. He had

7

said nothing else during the first three weeks of his stay at the hospital. He had obviously lost touch with reality, according to the psychologist in charge. Despite the delusional mannerisms, however, he had doggedly refused to take any medication, reluctantly began eating small portions of the food he had been served, especially savoring his morning bowl of cornflakes. As the weeks turned into months he had lapsed into a monk-like silence, following much of the daily routine without resistance.

"Ok, let's find out what's going on *after* we get there," the doctor chided himself for trying to predict the future.

The young doctor enjoyed the generally casual pace of his country practice. The typical ear, nose, and throat infections, the occasional cases of heart disease, serious enough, and the constant parade of farm injuries, usually lacerations and broken bones occupied most of his weekly schedule.

After eight years of schooling at the state university, the doctorial work, and his internship at the Cook County Hospital, the bright, motivated MD could have set up practice pretty much anywhere. But Richard Bowman knew he was a country boy at heart and had always felt a calling to serve the folks from the town where he had been born and raised.

He owned a nice house on State Street, three doors down from his parents' home. He had a woman, too. Since his senior year in high school he had toyed with the idea of marrying his long-time sweetheart, Ann Meyers, now a paralegal aid with a small office across from Brewer's hardware store. He often wondered why he kept getting cold feet when it came to tying the knot. She was attractive and witty. She was the perfect friend and confidant. Only a fool would think that she would wait forever. It had always seemed odd that a small, unshakable feeling, an uncertainty of the future, was conspiring to hold him back.

The desire to stick to his roots was further underscored by a two year tour of active duty halfway around the world. Richard's mind now began to dwell on some of the not-so-pleasant aspects of his young life. He found himself thinking about the turbulent times just after he had graduated from

8

college. As a National Guardsman, the twenty-seven year old had been unexpectedly ordered to the desolate desert regions of Iraq during the Desert Storm Offensive. There, he had worked under the sand camouflaged canvas of a triage tent, treating soldiers with wounds inflicted by the shrapnel of roadside bombs and the deadly lead slugs attributed to enemy and friendly fire alike. Mysterious illnesses that could only be explained by the unthinkable use of chemical warfare also crossed his path. He had treated civilians there, too. The groans and screams of the sick and wounded surfaced in his memory making his palms sweat as he gripped the steering wheel a little tighter. He recalled having wished there were more he could do to alleviate the pain and suffering he saw there. He had prayed for miracles more than once.

"Miracles," he mumbled to himself, "What the hell is a miracle, anyway?"

Upon his reunion with family and friends, he eagerly agreed to sign on with Dr. Watson, one of two local family practitioners in Winford. Six months before the doctor was to retire, without any obvious symptoms, the sixty-four-year-old man suffered a fatal stroke and quietly passed away in his sleep. His widow had always considered his young partner to be the grandson the couple had never had and implored him to keep her late husband's office operational. She gave him the small converted house and its contents and he had made her proud with his expertise and genuine concern for his patients. The practice had thrived over the past twelve years.

Something was lacking in Dr. Bowman's life, however. There was a restlessness he could never quite pin down. He knew people were born and died every day of the week. He had the power to patch some of them up but he often found himself struggling to give people hope. To a man of science, life was finite and fragile. Controlling all of the variables, he assumed, was impossible. Healing was a process with no guarantees. He knew for certain that he was not God.

Three years ago, on impulse, he had decided to take on an itinerant position at the Lincoln County Mental Health

Facility. It was in this roundabout way that the doctor envisioned himself getting to know more about the psyche of his fellow man, what hurt and what helped, the healing powers of the mind, the mysteries of the will to survive versus abject self-destruction.

He had told Annie that he needed a diversion, but he had also felt, in some small way, as if the assignment would serve as a penitence for a short, perhaps innocent enough role in an ever widening circle of war being waged, supposedly on his behalf by the U.S. Government. He hadn't personally pointed a gun and fired, but some of the soldiers he had helped recover from their own wounds certainly had. The dreams still haunted him. Helping people eased his conscience, at least a little. He knew he would never be able to change the world. How could one man ever hope to make such an impact?

The visiting doctor took notice of a small group of people that sat just outside the hospital gate. These so-called "followers" had been encamped in a wooded area near the institution's fenced-in compound since Jack's arrival six months ago. They were watching the car as it made its way up the drive to the gated entrance. One middle-aged woman held up a sign that read, "Free the Healer!" as he rolled slowly past.

He continued up to the electric gate spanning the brick archway and was quickly carded through. He rolled undisturbed into the staff parking area. Ignition off, he removed his attaché case and a white coat from the back seat, locked the car, and made his way into the long, two story, L-shaped brick building.

"Good morning Darlene," he greeted the young, pleasantly plump receptionist. The preoccupied employee casually looked up from yet another half-read paperback in her never-ending succession of Harlequin romance novels. She smiled; reading glasses perched on the end of her slightly upturned nose.

"Morning, Doctor Bowman," she echoed. "Mr. Harmond is waiting in room C-5. He said he would only see you. Dr. Stannis didn't seem to think he was sick, or anything. He wasn't sure what to make of the request so we just called it in. Jack seemed to know you were due out here today. Just said, 'I need to see Doc Bowman,' over and over. That was it."

The doctor nodded in acknowledgement and continued down the long hall, pausing briefly as a burly security guard unlocked a heavy metal door, punctuated only by a meshed, six inch by six inch Plexiglas window. He smiled as the doctor passed through.

Richard's footsteps padded softly as he walked across the smooth linoleum tiles, a checkerboard of black and white, beneath his feet. In the distance, a nurse pushed a medicine cart toward the day room; he could hear a TV game show in progress. As he drew nearer, he stopped for a moment and observed as a young, quiet-spoken orderly attempted to calm a man who was sitting on the floor, crying and rocking mechanically. A thin, yet attractive, lady with wild, unkempt blond hair stared out another shatter-proof window, this one larger and overlooking a garden below. Two men at a small, round table argued over a game of cards, while others sat in stackable plastic chairs, fixated on the caged and elevated television's small screen, absorbed in their dogmatic routine. Dr. Bowman moved on, turning left down the side corridor and opening the door to room C-5.

"Good morning Mr. Harmond, I heard you asked to see me."

Jack glanced up at the blue-eyed, sandy-haired, middle-aged man entering the room in what he considered to be the stereotypical long white coat with the stereotypical stethoscope hanging out of one pocket. Jack was glad most medical doctors were pretty much the same. He knew even the younger ones would have some sense of decency and at least listen and say "Uh huh," from time to time indicating a professional interest.

Jack had been to the doctor's office twice after old Doc Watson died about twelve years back. Both visits were annual checkups to appease insurance adjusters. He trusted the new school MD, now an occasional visitor, about as much as anyone. Jack had lived a long life without family or a lot of friends around. He liked most folks but didn't trust just anyone. He hoped he could still trust the good doctor.

Today, Jack Harmond knew it was time for him to confide in someone. He was sixty-nine going on seventeen. It was not so much his body that he was concerned about, as it was the secret in his soul that he was now feeling so compelled to reveal. He wanted to free himself of a burden, one that he had carried for six months to the day; one that weighed heavily upon his shoulders and threatened to break him like a tree in a winter's ice storm. And he couldn't share it with just anyone.

"How are you feeling today?" Doctor Bowman, like everyone else, knew about the Miracles. But unlike some of the others he reserved his skepticism and dealt only with the day-to-day reality of his patient's aches and pains. "How's the arthritis? I haven't heard a peep out of you for several months now."

"That's about right," the spindly, weathered figure returned in a low gravely voice. "It's about time I had a talk with someone and you seem to be keen enough on listening," He paused briefly then looked into the eyes of the young physician. "Doc, I need to talk to somebody about the whole thing. And I mean the whole thing. And I don't mean like talking to those reporter-types, the local head doctors, or that bevy of so-called spiritual gurus that swarmed my place a while back. I need to talk to somebody who'll listen so somethin' good'll come of it all."

Doctor Bowman glanced at his watch, which immediately irritated Jack. "No, never mind!" He started to stand up from the small black and chrome chair in which he had been waiting for the past thirty minutes. "I know you're busy," then he added truthfully, "and I'm just an old man wanting to talk."

"Jack," the doctor stood like a hunter fearing that his next move would spook his quarry. "Mr. Harmond," he said slowly, "It's ok. I *would* like to know how you're doing and what's on your mind. I drove all the way out here. It's nearly noon and actually, I've cleared my calendar for the next couple of hours. I've got time for you. Please," he gently laid his right hand on Jack's shoulder, coaxing him to remain seated and with the left, pulled a rolling stool underneath himself and sat. "What do you want to discuss?"

He, like many of his colleagues, was still looking for answers. Perhaps now he would hear the real secret behind the string of so-called miracles. Everyone wants a reasonable explanation for things that cannot easily be explained. Nearly two hundred people, pain free for over six months, seemed to fit that category. The doctor sat back, his elbow on the small computer desk behind him. The thought of finally getting to the truth of the matter was quite tantalizing. He was all ears.

"Do you believe in miracles, doc?" the old man's thin white hair and full beard formed a Gaussian halo around his lightly tanned and freckled face. He smiled and looked down sheepishly.

"Do you?" Dr. Bowman echoed.

"It may not be all that important what I think," Jack said a bit sarcastically. "But I reckon it's time I told somebody the whole story about everything that's happened. Ya know, I figured out pretty quick that most people will stab ya in the back and leave you for dead if they can get somethin' valuable out of you for nothin'. I know you probably don't understand, but the truth is, I've gotta trust somebody and Doc, you've always seemed like a straight arrow to me. I hope you're the kind of person I think you are."

Doctor Bowman sat up straighter on his examining stool. He looked squarely at Jack, sitting across from him and said, "Please go on."

"Well, you know me, Doc. As usual, I was out sitting up on Cemetery Ridge, just off the road so's I could get a clear view o' Winfield. I was with Red, you remember Red?" Jack's voice softened and was followed by a small sigh. "Anyways, we was sittin' up there watchin' this big storm blow in from the southwest. It was in April for sure, around the 8th, if I remember. That was just this past spring." He paused and

13

scratched his stubbly chin as if trying to remember something that had happened years ago.

"Me and Red, that's right," he finally continued, "we was sittin' in my '58 Chevy pickup, there at the top of the hill where we could see the better part of Winfield. A storm was comin' in from the southwest, as I said, and I could tell it was going to be a hummer. I figure major wind, rain, and o' course there was always the chance of a tornado, heaven forbid!"

Dr. Bowman listened intently, as Jack began to relate his recollection of the events. The good doctor resigned himself to patiently allow the old man's story to unfold.

Part 2

"Looks like a big one, don't it?" Red says, his eyes focused on the western sky.

"We'll get some work out of this one, that's for sure," Jack replied.

Jack, the tree doctor, had already begun the business of scanning the neatly laid out community below them. Streets, avenues, and lanes spiraled out from the crown of the hill like the fine threads of a spider's web. His eyes were especially focused on the larger trees outlining a four-block area bordered by State, Capital, Oak, and Main Streets. The dense green canopy looked like the walls of some lost and legendary fortress. A modest stream half encircled the base of the hill like a medieval moat running to the south. The old man looked over his left shoulder to check the big tree zone and would continue to do so every five minutes. They had the perfect vantage point.

A gust of wind hit the well maintained old truck causing it to rock and the radio antenna to rattle. It was only four o'clock in the afternoon but the headlights of the steel workhorse were already on and piercing the unusually early darkness that surrounded them. The misting rain that had been

14

blurring the windshield subsided. Jack flipped off the wipers and studied the sky above. The nose of the truck was pointed due west.

"What the hell is that?" Red was the first to see it.

Jack's eyes followed Red's pointing finger to the sky just northwest of the rural community. At first glance he thought that the warm white glow was the reflection of a release of electrical energy. However, the frequent, distant flashes of lightning on the southwestern horizon had just begun to announce the coming of the more severe weather from that direction. Only now were the two men beginning to hear the faint rumblings of the thunder that was accompanying those distant jagged-edged bolts.

But this light, off and to the northwest, was too far separated from the approaching front. And although the glow seemed to be appearing and disappearing into the clouds that thickened the sky, it did not flash as random bolts of lightning would. It was softer, and almost seemed spherical in shape. Jack would have easily dismissed it as an airplane, except for the fact that the light was not blinking. Airplane wing lights always blink, and usually red or blue. The forward runway lights would seldom be seen in an area so far distant from a major airport. The steady round luminous object appeared to be moving closer, perhaps a half a mile distant. Now, both Jack and Red were following the object's movement, almost hypnotized by its slow approach. Seconds turned into minutes.

An unexpected bolt of lightning struck close, followed by a huge crash of thunder. The approaching storm was now nearly overhead. So, too, was the glowing round entity. The two observers hugged the dashboard to better see the light that hovered above them. Suddenly, the orb broke up, dividing itself into three small, round, glowing objects, each shooting off in a different direction.

Jack was more shaken by this event than by the crackling thunder. Red's mouth dropped open. The two watched intently as one of the smaller objects rapidly fell towards the rural community. It was spinning in tight circles as

15

it dropped from the sky. Jack estimated it to be about four and a half feet in diameter as it disappeared into the treetops below them.

Jack was certain of its trajectory and the place of its ultimate impact. Oak Street was lined with the thick spring yellow-green hues of majestic old white oak trees, stately sycamores, and a handful of manicured maples, only a few blocks away. He pumped the clutch of the old Chevy truck and put it into first gear. It lurched forward.

"Did you see that?" Red was squinting upward to see if anything else would be falling from the cloud-choked sky.

Jack didn't bother answering. His mind was focused. Not only was he picturing the street, but the tree and very branches through which the object would have had to pass, twisting, snapping, and destroying them in the process. This was a chance to not only recover some artifact that had fallen from the sky, but also to be the first one on the scene to offer assistance to the property owner. It had to have passed through the thick canopy of trees down on Oak Street, he was almost dead sure of it. The truck veered right on Capital.

Red knew the routine. His hands tightly gripped the dashboard as the truck swerved onto the wet street and headed down the hill. Jack didn't bother putting on his turn signal or slowing up much for the left turn onto Oak Street. The truck neatly slid around the corner and continued to pick up speed. Red, keen with anticipation, imagined himself as some would-be emergency medical technician making an ambulance run to save some poor soul. Jack would get them both safely to the scene where the fallen victim would await them.

All of 19, Red greatly admired Jack and his love for the trees. His respect for Jack manifested itself in his wearing of the same plaid wool work shirts, blue jeans, and khaki ball cap every day they worked together. He liked to watch as Jack studied each tree, considering it as though it were an individual with its own personality. He would walk up to them, saying things like "How ya doing today?" Or "what's the matter, aren't ya feelin' good today?" With the skills of a surgeon, Jack would slowly climb up into the branches, inspect them carefully, and then instruct Red to cut away only what was necessary. He would tend the cuts and scrapes too, and work to cure all sorts of diseases and infestations. When he finished he'd always look back over his shoulder and say, "Now that didn't hurt much, did it?"

Jack had a great bedside manner with the trees' owners, as well. He would carefully explain what needed to be done and when the individual he spoke with was intent on doing too much or not enough, he would very carefully explain again why it had to be done just so and nine times out of ten, end up doing it just that way. Everybody that ever had a need to cut down or save a tree in Winfield knew Jack. It was almost as if he would magically appear on their doorsteps before they even had the chance to consult their pocket smart-phones. He would often be seen leaning from the window of that antique forest green pickup truck, talking with people out in their front yards while they were raking leaves or planting flowers. He would remind them to look after the trees. "They live and breath, eat and drink, same as the rest of us," he'd say in his casual tone.

The truck slowed up when the inevitable wall of rain forced the old man to flip on the windshield wipers. As they crossed State Street and entered the 800 block of Oak, Jack's eyes were on the left hand side, mid-block, intently searching for signs of damage on the ground. The full force of the intense spring deluge was now upon them. Both simultaneously rolled down windows to get a clearer view. Across the street a plastic garbage pail tumbled across Mr. Evert's side yard. The tops of trees swayed and you could hear the moaning of the old branches, as they resisted the forty mile an hour gusts.

"I don't see nothin' do you?" Red stated the obvious.

"Nothin', Red, you're right," Jack mumbled.

Another fierce crackle of white light slammed into a house-top lightning rod the next block over. The roar that followed had both men pulling their elbows and heads back inside the truck. The branches above them now danced about like marionettes on a string. The pickup rolled on at a snail's pace. There was still no sign of the mysterious light or an obvious point of impact. Jack was shaking his head and mumbling to himself. The truck stopped briefly as he pulled his ball cap off and wiped the rain from his face with his weathered hand.

The melodic chime of the cell phone at his waist alerted him to an incoming call.

"Jack here," he raised his voice to be heard over the sounds of the truck's engine and wind blowing fiercely outside his open window. "What can I do ya fer?"

He listened intently for a minute or two then flipped his not-so-smart phone shut and stepped on the accelerator. They took the first right, heading down toward Stone Creek. Just short of Main Street the truck slid to an abrupt halt. A shallow-rooted pine created a barrier across the road in front of them.

Jack waved to a man standing inside a front porch enclosure. He and Red did a fireman's dismount from the vehicle. Both circled to the back on opposite sides of the truck. The apprentice mechanically flipped down the tailgate and lifted the back hatch of the camper cover protecting their equipment. Jack reached in grabbing a small chainsaw and pulled it from its resting place.

In a seemingly well-rehearsed exercise, the two men began to dissect the fallen tree and remove it piece by piece to the side of the road. The task took no more than 10 minutes.

"I'll be around to collect tomorrow!" Jack yelled back towards the man on the porch. The man waved back.

For the next three hours Red and Jack made their way up and down every street within a five-mile radius of the hill. Time and again they came upon fallen limbs and uprooted trees, seeking permission in each case to assist the homeowner's involved; they worked as they were given the ok to do so. Red carefully recorded each location and what had been done, making entries in a small, red notebook. He knew Jack was a trusting man and would expect compensation in the coming days. It was the way he'd always done business during the busy times.

On several occasions Jack circled back around to check the 800 block of Oak Street. Each time he closely inspected the trees as they drove under them. He was especially intent on studying a big oak in the middle of the block. Once, Red caught him mumbling something to himself, and an "I'll be danged!"

About eight o'clock that night the storm had pretty much blown itself out. Jack dropped Red at his house and the forest green truck disappeared into the darkness.

Jack lived about five miles outside of Winfield. Red's farm was out two miles beyond his place. Once again passing his own small well-kept cottage, flanked by two majestic trees, the old man had his mind set on one last run to Oak Street. This time, as he arrived in the concealing darkness, he switched off the Chevy's engine and sat in the stillness of the cab. The two had gone up and down all of the adjacent streets and had seen no signs of the mysterious object's impact anywhere. But he was dead certain that the small globe had landed here. He strained his eyes looking up into the thick graceful branches of the ancient white oak. Something was different about one branch in particular, something that began to bother him. He couldn't quite manage to sort it out, however, and finally gave up. Anyway, it was too dark to do anything about it now. Reluctantly, he fired up the six cylinder engine and headed for home.

The next day was busier than the night before. As usual, with one of the first big storms of the season, everybody decided all at once that they needed old limbs cut away that threatened houses and sheds. Red even had to employ the use of Jack's second vehicle, a shiny blue Ford 150 pickup truck, to haul off some of the cut wood. Jack was funny. He had bought the truck but seldom drove it. Red never understood why. But he did know that Jack seldom did anything without a good reason.

Jack had a fireplace at his house and never had a shortage of firewood. It was all neatly stacked in ricks behind the small brown and white cottage. Storms like this one paid off in more than one way. Even if the tree's owner didn't reimburse him, at least somewhere down the line, he knew he'd have a warm winter. And Red knew if his family ever needed wood for their stove, Jack would be the first to share his.

Red made three trips to the house that day. The work was hard and the day went fast for the both of them.

The next day was Sunday. Jack didn't see himself as a religious man. But he thought of himself as a spiritual person. He believed in God more than he believed in the words of men. God was all around him every day, as far as he was concerned. There was no need for attending a church to remind him of the powers of the Creator. The Good Lord's work was everywhere he looked, especially in the trees.

Jack spent the morning checking the oil in his trucks and cleaning his tools. He was especially careful to check the climbing gear, ropes, pulleys, cleats, and the rest. He was a cautious man when it came to climbing trees. In his day he had worked from some of the most precarious places, perched in branches thirty, sixty, even ninety feet above the ground.

Jack was moving slower than usual these days. He knew he was getting too old for this type of work; his arms and legs ached from a slow creeping arthritis that threatened to put an end to it all. Several years ago he had talked to Doc Bowman about it and was told that he would simply have to learn to live with it. Time could not be turned back, nor youth regained. Jack spoke to his God about his discomfort, never complaining, but looking for a little relief from the nagging pain now and then. If he would tend God's creation all of his life, he felt it was the least God could do to repay him. Jack's biggest fear was not being able to get up and go to work when the time came.

After his noon meal, Jack decided to take a leisurely drive. He did have a destination; he was not fooling himself or anyone else for that matter. He headed his trusty Chevy towards the small community and the biggest tree on Oak Street. When he got there he went directly to the door and knocked hard three times. He could hear the faint scooting of a walker and patiently waited until Mrs. Orber appeared at the door, cautiously opening it ever so slightly.

"Afternoon, Mrs. Orber," Jack quickly pulled his cap from his head of wispy gray hair. "Mind if I have a word with you?"

"Not at all, Jack." She had gone to high school with him and knew him well. "Come on in…" She pulled the door open.

"I don't have much time," Jack returned, not wishing to turn this into a social visit. "It's about your tree, the big oak; I have a favor to ask."

Mrs. Orber smiled and waited for him to continue. She knew he was a shy sort of fellow and didn't want to press him.

"Well, you remember me taking out that limb that was gonna swing low over the roadway about ten years ago don't ya? Well," Jack didn't want to appear to be soliciting work or worrisome about his visit, "Well, with the storm and all the other day, I was wondering if I couldn't check out that big branch we took her off of, ya know, see if she's holdin' up alright. I won't charge ya nothin'. I just wanna to see if she's holdin' up alright," he repeated himself nervously. "If it's ok with you, I'll shimmy up there and take a look. Would that be alright?" Now he was beginning to feel like a schoolboy asking for a date. He blushed self-consciously. "Won't take but a few minutes."

"Sure, Jack. You go right ahead," Mrs. Orber smiled and waved him on. Jack didn't hesitate. He quickly walked back to his truck and unfastened the aluminum ladder from the topside of the camper shell. Carefully he maneuvered it, placing it at the base of the tree near the sidewalk and gingerly leaned it against the giant oak. His heart was pounding.

He had been dying to get up into that old tree since the night of the storm. It was as if he thought she could tell him something about the strange glowing objects. Before ascending Jack put on his climbing spikes and prepared a rope for the ascent into the higher branches. Mentally he checked his preparations as he went on with them. He did not want to be in such a hurry that he would end up falling and injuring himself. By now this was a part of a routine that he seldom gave a second thought.

Once at the top of the ladder Jack secured one end of a thick nylon rope about his waist and taking careful aim flung the coiled remainder over a large branch just above where he stood. His shoulder ached with this action and he paused to rub it. It was hurting him pretty bad today. But this was not to deter him. He reached out and grabbed the rope's end that now dangled from the tree limb. He quickly threaded it through a belay device strapped to a climbing belt that would support him as he pulled his way up. Taking up the slack he began moving upward, checking his weight against the downward sway of the limb above as he went.

He was over fifteen feet up when he pulled himself across the face of the tree to the street side. He now swung freely just beneath a great branch that arced over the street below.

Curiously he studied the limb, his eyes meticulously running up and down the underside of the thick black arm. It appeared smooth and undamaged. As he scanned it, he noticed that the entire tree appeared strong and healthy. There were no broken branches here, no nicks, blemishes, or even the outlines of the typical hollow left behind after a limb has been removed. The latter observation was by far the most disconcerting since Jack had personally cut and patched a severed branch at this very spot. There was no sign of the event, no sign at all! But that was impossible. This tree or any other tree would always carry such scars. He was beginning to second-guess his own memory.

Jack began talking to himself as he often did in the seclusion of the trees. He came right out and said, 'What's goin' on here? What happened to your scar? Where'd it go?"

The tree's leaves rustled in the breeze in a soft whisper. Jack sensed she was healthy and quite happy. He was the one with the problem. Jack reached into the pocket of his jeans and pulled out his Barlow. Opening it up, he spoke again, "Now this won't hurt but a tiny bit."

In a slow, careful action he ran the sharp blade of his knife into the tough bark just above his dangling position. He had consciously been keeping an eye on this part of the branch over the past several years. There was always the possibility of bug infestation, something that can easily follow the cutting away of a piece of any tree. But today there was no sign of the previous knot or the oval lip-like swell around it.

The ancient tree seemed to resist the knife's penetration. The blade's tip sank only to a depth of a quarter of an inch and no more. He moved it downward and toward himself, cutting a seam about three inches in length, then removed it, folded the blade and placed it back into his pocket.

Jack couldn't keep from shaking his head in amazement. "Don't that beat all?"

Again he looked up into the branches and wished that she could explain this mystery to him. All was quiet.

Just as Jack was beginning to prepare for his decent, a droplet of pinkish liquid oozed out of the fresh cut in the bark. It hung for an instant and then let go, falling the few inches between the tree and the right shoulder of his green and blue plaid shirt collar. Jack felt the substance hit and instinctively reached his left hand over to wipe it off. The stuff felt like sap and when he rubbed his thumb against his fingers, it spread itself over them and clung in the same tenacious manner. He resorted to wiping them on his jeans and thought no more of it.

Ten minutes later in his descent from the tree, it occurred to Jack that the climb down was always easier than the climb up. And before he hit the ground the old man found himself smiling and feeling as though he had just risen from a long and deep sleep. He was refreshed and ready to do anything. In his usual fashion he carefully removed his climbing equipment, stowing each item in its proper place. Then he re-coiled the rope and having placed it inside, carefully closed up the camper.

Finally, he placed the ladder back on the top of the truck and secured it firmly. Offhandedly he wondered why he didn't seem to be bothered by the aches and pains that had beset him less than an hour ago.

Still not sure what to make of it he reluctantly went back up to the house and knocked on the door a second time.

"Just wanted to let you know that your oak is fine and dandy," he quipped. Mrs. Orber had come to the door balancing a small tin of cookies on her walker basket. She smiled to see him so contented with his efforts.

"Have a cookie, Jack," she invited. He reached around the partially opened door and into the tin with his right hand and retrieved one. Then, in his usual pleasant manner he reached out with his left hand and touched the top of her extended arm.

"Thank you!" he said sincerely and turned to make his way back to his truck and his own small field of trees.

* * * * *

Back in the white-walled office, Doc Bowman shifted nervously in his seat as Jack paused briefly from his narrative. He knew the idea of some plant, or combination of plant and insect secretion with medical properties was not out of the question. He had the sudden urge to abandon the old man and round up a team to analyze every inch of the ancient tree in Mrs. Orber's front yard. He eyed Jack tentatively, carefully concealing the ever-growing urge to usurp the old man's position as a so-called healer. A doctor of medicine could find a great deal of fame in such a discovery. And the world would be better for it, not leaning on theological superstition, instead embracing the true laws of nature and science.

The eyes of the two men met. Doctor Bowman realized there might be more to the magical cure than just tree sap. He settled himself reluctantly and said, "Yes, go on."

"I slept like a baby that night, Jack continued. I woke at the crack of dawn and rolled out of bed and did my usual morning stretch, just like you told me to do last year."

Jack was beginning to perceive the doctor's impatience. He spoke with a quiet urgency now, hoping that he would be able to convey the entire story without losing the physician's interest.

"I felt good, really good," Mr. Harmond went on without further urging. Richard Bowman's gaze fell to the floor as the tale resumed.

Part 3

Jack plodded into the kitchen and poured himself a bowl of Corn Flakes.

"Cornflakes have got to be the best food on earth!" the Midwesterner said to himself as he launched into the morning bowl. He was picturing himself an athlete, getting ready to hurl a javelin or discus across an Olympic field. Those guys always end up on a cereal box cover. I should 'a tried harder at track back in my school days, he smiled to himself at the thought. Ah, but I was always so shy. I would have had a hard time being a jock. "Naaah," he chuckled at his own little joke to himself.

Jack liked reaching back into his past like that, picturing himself young again and full of life and energy. He had always wished he were more popular with the girls. But today he felt like he could actually be there and be doing it his way. He felt an inner glow like nothing before. It was almost eerie. He grabbed an apple from a bowl on the table and began eating it.

When he was finished he rinsed the empty bowl and spoon in the sink and put them up to dry in the dish drainer. He set the apple's core aside to be later thrown on top of the compost heap.

Looking out his kitchen window he surveyed his backyard. Beyond the yard, next to the shed was a good-sized vegetable garden. Some of the newly planted starts were beginning to leaf up. He had planted individual rows of carrots, squash, onions, some pole beans, head lettuce, and watermelon. He also planted some tomatoes and potatoes along the side of his tool shed just behind the compost pile when the seasons allowed.

On the far side of the garden grew his favorite treasures. He had carefully planted, pruned, and harvested each of the twenty different trees for the past forty-seven years. They were short and tall, thick and thin, all in neatly aligned rows, rising from the unkempt crabgrass that was just beginning to green up from the winter's killing frost. He especially liked the fruit. His orchard included five types of apples including Granny Smiths and Fujis, Bosc and red pears, apricots, lemons, cherries, and plums, just to name a few.

The site was also home to walnut, hickory nut, and a couple of South American nut trees that grew simply to acknowledge what he called his nutty side. If it grew on trees and you could eat it, it belonged in his arboreal paradise on earth. He liked the whole of it. He loved the smell of fresh picked fruit and didn't mind getting his hands roughed up or dirty. He smiled to himself as he recalled having planted thousands of seedlings across at least five local counties in years gone by. It had been a labor of love. He looked down at his hands and studied them intently.

In the front yard, two of the area's tallest and longest standing sycamore trees stood proudly flanking the right and left sides of the small wood framed house. Well over 100 years old, the European natives' broad leaved branches blocked wind and rain, as well as summer sun. He could see the shadows of their branches being cast far into the backyard from the rays of the morning sun. These were his ninety-foot guardians. They watched over the place and made it home.

He loved the idea that a tree could outlive a man. It was only right that God would humble the human being in this way. We are foolish to think we are the biggest or the best of all things created, he reckoned. We were meant to be caretakers, that was all, and nothing more.

Back inside the tidy cottage, Jack headed for the bathroom. The door was open wide and the mirror above the sink caught his reflection as it did every morning. Jack saw himself smiling. He stared deep into his own eyes as he approached. This past winter had been pretty rough on account of the arthritis that had been getting him down. There had not been too many mornings when that smile had appeared, at least not this early in the day.

As Jack took to the task of shaving he noticed that an old scar, a scrape from a run-in with a hickory tree, he used to say, had faded to blend in with the surrounding skin. He rubbed at the place and then continued shaving. His skin seemed tight and less wrinkled than usual. It was obvious that last night's sleep had done him a world of good.

After dressing in his usual attire Jack got on the phone and called Red's house. As usual Red's mother, Martha, answered the phone.

"Hey, Jack, how are you doin' this morning?" Martha was a long time country girl who had been absorbed into the growing bedroom community by default. She was a widow of six years now and had almost single-handedly held down the Jackson farm for the sake of a fifth generation. Over the years parcels of land had been sold off when times were hard and now only a ten acre tract with an old run down barn remained. A handful of chickens and a couple of pigs made up the entirety of the livestock and a three quarter acre truck garden provided fresh vegetables just about all year 'round. Jack had helped Red and Bill, his younger brother, plant some fruit trees, three varieties of apple, there last summer.

Martha liked to gossip and got in as many "Did you hears...?" as she could before Red took over the phone. Usually Jack held the phone slightly away from his ear during this prelude to her son's morning salutation. Today however, one name caught his attention.

"Did you hear about Mrs. Orber? Well Virginia, my friend from church said that her cousin Linda Brighten, you know, Mrs. Orber's daughter, before she married that Brighten boy, Jeff, well anyhow, she said that her Mother was a sight to see this mornin'. You know that old lady put down her walker and all them fancy canes and walked the four blocks over to Linda's house just to have morning coffee! Can you imagine? She hadn't been out of that house for nearly four years! Isn't that the strangest thing you ever heard, Jack?" She didn't really wait for an answer but continued the local news bulletin until he heard Red's voice asking her to give up the phone.

"Sorry Jack," he apologized, "Didn't mean to keep you waiting so long."

"It's ok, boy, are ya ready to roll?

"Sure Jack, I'll be waitin' out front when you get here,"

The phone business being completed, Jack hung up the receiver of the antique dial phone that still graced an old lamp table in the narrow hallway. The old man methodically patted his belt above his right pocket and went straight to the bedroom to retrieve the cell phone on the dresser. Clipping it on securely, he was on his way.

Jack was glad that the spring weather had finally settled in. The greening up of the Indiana countryside was evident all around him as he made his way to his apprentice's two-story farm house.

It had been a long winter for Red's family. The early snows in November had cut short any garden work, as well as, the tree trimming business. The three inhabitants of the O'Malley farm had pretty much been living on canned goods, their laying hens' eggs, and one butchered hog for the better part of four months.

Red had already begun tilling and planting his family's truck garden in the evenings. Jack knew his mother would be happy to see the sprouts coming up for air in a week or two. He also knew that it meant a longer day for his young sidekick, but his brother Billy, who just turned fourteen, was becoming ever-the-more helpful, and the season ahead promised to be a good one.

About ten minutes later Jack showed up in a cloud of dust as his pickup ground to a halt. Red stood waiting at the edge of the circular driveway, as was his custom in good weather. He must have noticed how relaxed, almost carefree Jack appeared this morning. He climbed into the cab.

"What's up?" Red quipped.

"What's up yourself?" Jack countered in a joking fashion. Red wasn't sure how to take the offhand reply so he quickly opened the small ledger he'd been clutching. The pocket-sized notebook served as schedule and collection book. Jack liked Red's ability to keep track of each day's business.

"Uh, I guess we need to check in with Mr. Gruber. Remember him talkin' about clearing that half-acre over by the new schoolhouse? He's gonna set it up to sell lots for a couple of houses, I guess."

Jack rolled his eyes. He didn't care much for development. This would be a challenge. He knew he was going to have to practically beg Mr. Gruber to save a single tree on that property. And there were some beauties. Last he remembered, there were two graceful weeping willows bowing over Stone Creek. A handful of hickories grew toward the far end of the lot, down toward the water's edge, as well. And there were a pair of pin oaks, ten feet apart, both nearly fifty feet tall that John Gruber's own father had left standing after clearing the land for grazing some years back. The two "old soldiers," as Jack saw them, were steadfastly standing at attention near the center of the property. At least five other trees, mostly wild saplings were scattered around the half acre field, as well.

"Alright, let's see what we can do for the trees today," Jack said with a manner of confidence.

Two and a half hours later the three men made their way back down the slope to a narrow gravel road that ran beside a pleasantly gurgling stream. A compromise was all Jack could come away with on this occasion. Mr. Gruber had reluctantly agreed to extend the gravel access road ten feet further up from the creek bed, allowing the willows to stay. But he insisted that the walnut trees be felled, saying that every year it was just a big mess to clean up. He spared a small sassafras tree and two slick elms, but only if Jack gave him a discount on transplanting them to the edges of the lot. The others did not share the same fate. And finally, to Jack's absolute dismay, Mr. Gruber insisted that at least one of the twin oaks would have to be cut to the ground.

Jack's cheerful optimism diminished as he realized one of the guardian trees would have to go on without its mate. "They've stood together for so long, it'd be such a shame..." he implored.

"Sorry Jack, one tree between the houses will be plenty of shade," The owner had made up his mind. "You can decide which will stay and which will go, how's that?"

Jack sucked in his breath and held it. Red knew the meaning of this act. Jack would rather die himself than choose which tree would live and which would be felled. He held the breath as a way to calm himself. Then he slowly exhaled and replied, "No, Mr. Gruber, you decide and I'll take care of it." Jack didn't much care for the role of executioner either, but at least this way his conscience was clear.

Jack, for his part, would make certain that any tree he cut down did not get cast off before taking into consideration its other potential contributions. When possible he carefully preserved the wood for those cutting or carving it into useful products or works of art. He knew every lumber mill in the state and the types of wood they specialized in cutting and preparing for use. He knew a lot of woodsmen too, folks who worked with chainsaws and hand tools in their craft. He especially liked people who saw the angels in the wood and worked to free them.

As the two climbed into the Chevy, Jack called out to the departing man, "We'll start first thing Thursday morning and should have things ready for you in about two weeks, ok?"

"Sounds good, Jack," the pudgy landowner's voice trailed off as the truck rattled across a one-lane bridge spanning the creek.

Jack and Red spent the better part of the rest of the day going back to collect on jobs done during the previous week. And, as usual Jack was always scouting for potential work. Once when they were close to the Orber house Jack was tempted to verify the strange story he had heard earlier that morning but at the last minute decided against it.

"It'll wait," he thought to himself. "Besides, that would be a *miracle* if it were true!"

Back at home that evening the self-appointed caretaker of the trees again found himself staring into the bathroom mirror. For a brief moment he even imagined that the gray hair on his head had gotten one shade darker. Jack was tired, but with no simple explanation, he still felt good. He breathed in deeply, exhaled slowly, and then shook his head as he walked away.

When he finished cleaning up from his supper the old man went out into the back yard to sit in a faded white straight-backed wooden kitchen chair. He withdrew the Barlow knife from his pocket. Anticipating a pale blue and pink-pastel sunset he unsheathed the blade and picked out a small stick from the woodpile to whittle. He never carved much more than tender wood and chips for kindling, but the task served to pass the time. Just as he was about to begin he took note of a thin but sticky pinkish substance that coated the blade. Pressing his thumb and forefinger tight to each side of the metal he tried his best to wipe the surface clean, and then wiped the residue carelessly on the leg of his jeans once more. Having done this, he did his best to clear his mind and get down to the business of putting a point on the end of the stick.

Jack had made considerable progress on creating a small pile of shavings when the telephone in the hall began ringing. It was not unlike people to call at all odd hours to let him know they had something for him to do. He got to the phone at the tail end of the sixth ring and pulled it up to his ear.

"What can I do ya fer?"

"Hello, Jack?" The voice on the other end was familiar and female. "Jack, it's me, Mary Orbers!"

Jack wasn't at all sure how to reply so he just stood and listened.

"Are you there, Jack?" Her voice sounded giddy.

"Yea, I'm here," he finally responded.

"Jack," now her voice was soft, as if to whisper a secret, "you did something to me. You took away the pain, Jack. It's

31

gone, and it happened just after you touched me yesterday afternoon. Jack, it's a miracle!"

"Mrs. Orber…"

"Call me Mary," the voice at the other end of the line insisted.

Jack blushed and was glad no one was there to see him do it. "Uh, er, Mary, what in tarnation are you goin' on about?"

"I don't know what else to think, Jack. You know I've had the most awful time with my back problems, and after my bypass surgery, why I never thought I was goin' to have a moment's comfort from that time on. But I feel fine today. No, more than that, Jack, I, I feel good, really good! In fact, I feel as though I could go dancin' in the moonlight!"

Jack lowered the phone from his ear for a minute not quite able to envision his old school mate dancing anywhere, let alone in the moonlight. He didn't want to appear rude however, and put the receiver back to his ear hoping she had not noticed his absence.

"Why you think I had anything to do with it?" Jack finally mustered the courage to ask.

"It happened right after you touched me, Jack. I wouldn't lie, it really did! Couldn't've been more than a half'n hour after that. I haven't told a soul though. I mean, I have let on that I'm feelin' so much better but I haven't told anyone that it was you that did this thing,"

"It wasn't me, Mrs… I mean, Mary. It couldn't've been me. I'm just the tree man. I ain't no doctor or nothin'.

"All I know is what I know," Mary insisted. "I won't tell anybody if you don't want me to, but I just had to call and say thank you, for whatever you did and for what ever reasons. Thank you, Jack, thank you so much!" He could hear the sounds of a woman stifling her tears and repositioned the phone to the other side of his head, uneasily.

"Mary, I don't know what to say, but don't go 'round tellin' anybody it was me that made you all better. It must've been something good ya done that you was blest for. Thank your lucky stars and take care of yourself. I…, I gotta go now; I've got something on the stove. Bye now, you take care."

The words "Thank you. Thank you, Jack…" faded as he put the phone back in its cradle.

Jack was completely unnerved by the conversation. For the first time in a very long time he went into the kitchen and reached up on the top shelf above the sink and pulled down a fifth of Kentucky bourbon whiskey. The bottle was generally reserved for times when he was down with the chills. He unscrewed the cap, pulled a large swig, and spun the cap back in place. The liquor burned its way down into his chest as he placed the bottle back in the cabinet. It served as a punch in the gut, reminding him of the existence of his own physical being. He was alive and he was awake, of that much he was sure.

The would-be healer breathed in slowly and deeply to center himself. He studied the relationship between the air and his own finite life, knowing full well that one thing is dependent upon the other, then exhaled silently. This was no dream. Something had happened. Something within him had changed. He was now certain of it.

Mentally he examined himself from head to toe. It felt as though all was right with the world. The constant pain deep within his arms and legs that had been a companion for so many years was gone. But there was something else. There was this energy, an energy he could clearly recall from his traveling days, back when he was in his early twenties. He wasn't quite sure if it was an energy born of optimism or simply optimism riding the wings of this unbelievable change. For the first time in a very long time it felt good to be alive!

Jack was also pleased that his gut feeling had given rise to the hope that was now verified by Mrs. Orber. Something real, something powerful had happened. But this same realization simultaneously sent a chill down his spine, like the workings of a cold wind on an All Hallows Eve. Something big had happened, all right. It was a change like no other he could recall. And this change was not natural. Not only that, but this power could affect people he touched. This was something incredible! How? Why? He looked down at his two callused and timeworn hands. The hands were still old but the calluses seemed to have softened. Silently he shook his head.

All his inner whispers began to run together. United they created a swift flowing torrent that now roared, "The tree, the tree the tree, THE TREE, THE TREE, THE TREE!"

There *was* something about that old oak; the power it held could not be explained away. He suddenly realized the stickiness of his right thumb and forefinger, still slightly moist from the thick pink sap that he had wiped from the blade of his Barlow just minutes ago. He looked down at his two digits intently, as if he might somehow be given a reason for everything that was happening. There was no reason, none, except the faint possibility that a soft white light had, indeed, found shelter in the limbs of that tree. And having done so had left something there for others to touch, to explore, to understand... to use. Jack Harmond had found it. Jack Harmond had used the power.

Part 4

Jack liked to be able to explain things, both to himself and then to others. He believed in the unseen worlds of spirits and angels but often caught himself reasoning through their acts. He imagined that good people attracted good energies, good spirits to themselves. Men with evil hearts sought out the demons that they would hope to tame and use to better their positions. Those same demons ultimately would, by their very nature, turn against their would-be masters and destroy them in the end.

Jack reasoned that only certain things could be seen and heard. After all, how would anyone in Winfield know if a child might be crying in some cold thatched hut in Outer Mongolia at this very moment? Similarly, how would one know if the hand of God had touched them? We all have our strengths and we all have our limitations. At least in this lifetime we must realize that we will never be able to know and understand all things possible, he reasoned. And yet, Jack would be sitting right up front if someone were to be discussing how a giant Sequoia might have managed to survive fire and pestilence, drought and flood, to exist nearly two thousand years in time.

Today Jack wished he could speak with a shaman. If only he knew of some wise ancient, some guru-type waiting to reveal the secrets of God and Nature; waiting for the right question. What would he ask? What would his question be?

"I'd sure like to know if the healing power really does come from that pink sap. What's it really do to you? If it heals you, will it last forever? Will it make you invincible, like Superman? Will the power to heal stay after the sap is gone? Did the glowing light have anything to do with the pink sap? Where did that glowing light come from anyway? And what am I supposed to do with this whole kettle of fish?"

The more questions that formed themselves in his mind the more overwhelmed he felt. There were too many unanswerable questions. He could not see into the unknown. No one would come forward to explain it to him.

Why had he been given this substance? Was it a matter of luck? He knew that others had probably seen the lights. Red had seen them! He wondered how many had sought to track them down, like the gold at the end of a rainbow. Perhaps the idea was just as foolish as the wishful thinking of an old Irish storyteller.

Yet Jack, the tree doctor, had gone looking. And it was Jack, alone, who had noticed the subtle change in the old oak that had further sparked his curious mind. He was the one with the spunk and the equipment to scale the height that brought him to the reservoir of the miracle producing substance. He was the one who would pass it on to another human, even if by accident. Why Jack? Why the tree doctor?

"Why me?" Jack heard the words manifest themselves in his lungs, push up through his throat, pass over his tongue, and leap out beyond his lips. This was his question!

He looked around himself. The house in which he lived was not much more than four walls and a roof. He was not surrounded by family and had few friends. He lived a simple life. It was all that he seemed to need. Did he need a pocketful of miracles? Did he deserve even one?

At sixty-nine, Jack had done his share of traveling. He had seen different lands, different people, and different cultures. He took each for what it had to offer and on a day not unlike any other he made a decision to return to his homeland, this place of his own ancestors, to settle down. The region was a land of trees and the trees became his fascination and his vocation. He studied them. He planted and grew them. He pruned and trimmed them. He healed them when he could. Now the trees came bearing this wondrous gift. Was it just a coincidence?

Another chill ran down his spine. This one made him shiver and move mechanically towards the small fireplace in the living room. Kneeling on the hearth he pulled a handful of shavings from an old bucket and scattered them neatly across the surface of a still warm bed of embers. Next he took a handful of dried sticks from a metal box just to the right of the fireplace and carefully stacked the kindling wood so that the air could draw in and around it. Leaning his face in and down toward the center of the pile he began blowing softly and once again brought life to tiny dancing flames. As the fire spread he carefully placed two small and then two bigger logs of hickory criss-crossed on top of the stack.

Jack brushed his knees, savored the sweet smoky odor, rose to his feet, and retreated to the old rocking chair that was always nearby. He spent the rest of the evening tending the fire, watching the flames, and staring into the fire's heart, hoping for answers.

As if a hand on his shoulder had shaken him awake, Jack's head suddenly jumped from his chest and his eyes squinted in the soft glow of the still burning fire. His vision cleared enough to see the big windup clock on the fireplace mantle. It was three thirty in the morning.

Recognizing it as a good omen, Jack was pleased by the circumstances. He wasn't sure if he had been dreaming or if the thoughts that now entered his head were sparked by the moment. Regardless, he knew it was time for action.

Jack pushed himself up from the rocker and walked through the silent house. He grabbed his corduroy jacket from a coat hook in the central hall as he made his way out the backdoor and into the faint light of a crescent moon high overhead. The conditions were perfect. Jack checked his pocket and withdrew the keys to his truck.

Minutes later he was headed for town. The truck, hugging the right side of the county road, wove its way through newly plowed fields that were just beginning to green with the sprouts of row upon row of corn or soybeans. He passed through patches of woods that usually topped hills or announced the presence of a spring or small creek bed nearby. A house and a barn or shed here and there gave way to clusters of houses and streets with little white signs, marking the edge of the larger community ahead. Finally the skyline took on the greenish-white glow of civilization as Winfield appeared on the horizon.

Jack had had a revelation. The consternation it caused him pushed him forward in this secretive act. It was obvious to him that he could never tell anyone about the source of the healing substance. If he did, the beautiful tree that graced the 800 block of Oak Street would surely be felled, carted off, studied, and probably sold to the highest bidder. And how many other trees would suffer the same fate in the frenzy of healing fever? He shook his head trying to push away the image of a barren land, devoid of its previously living, arboreal inhabitants.

But there was another element to Jack's vision. If he had been chosen to find the healing substance, would he be

37

forsaking some greater responsibility by simply ignoring its existence? One part of him was keenly aware of the potential for disaster that he could be embracing. Another part of him almost exploded with the excitement of being able to possess something that could change the world! Regardless of the outcome, his knowledge must be acted upon.

In the pre-dawn darkness, the faithful pickup rolled to a halt, engine stilled at the far end of the block to avoid attention. Jack repeated the ladder and rope climbing exercise in the darkness, this time almost effortlessly. Soon he found himself beneath the underside of the great oak limb.

In his rush to act upon his impulse, Jack had failed to think about bringing a normal container. Almost frantically he had searched through his truck for an old jar with a lid or a plastic container, but to no avail. He was about to give up when he spotted an empty sandwich bag on the floor of the truck cab. As it turned out, it was just what he needed. He had quickly stuffed it into his jacket pocket and now withdrew it for the task at hand.

Using the tips of his fingers he moved them across the rough bark trying in vain to detect the faint crease left by the incision he had made on his last visit to this spot. The cut was gone.

With Barlow and baggie in hand he made a fresh incision in the rough bark and patiently waited for the liquid to appear. Very much aware of the time and the possibility of discovery he began trying to coax the sap out by whispering, "Come on, come on…"

"Thank you," he then whispered to the tree and the Powers That Be as the pink substance began to drip from the branch.

Jack had been in the tree for nearly twenty minutes now. The sap had only filled the bottom of the bag, taking the space of a fat crayon or a roll of dimes. Jack knew he could not afford to be greedy. He sealed the bag and stuffed it back into his jacket pocket. This time, he withdrew a small tin of tar from his back pocket and using his finger smoothed it carefully into the groove, sealing it and making it invisible to eyes below. A dog barked in the distance and he held his breath.

It was only after the Chevy's engine kicked in and the vehicle neared the end of the 800 block that Jack actually felt himself breathing again. He looked into his rearview and side view mirrors cautiously, seeing no one behind him. The street was quiet. His mission was a success. The truck and its elflike driver made their way down the road and back out to the country.

Once home, Jack felt the weight of a sleepless night begin to take hold. He carefully placed the tightly sealed plastic bag in the bottom drawer of his dresser, under a pile of faded blue jeans. Yawning, he changed into his pajamas and crawled into bed. He was asleep as soon as his head hit the pillow.

He knew that things were strangely out of sync when he heard the continuous jangling of the phone in the distant hallway. Usually, he would be up and going before anyone would be calling in. He glanced toward the dresser, half remembering the dreamlike episode of the previous night. The phone, however, demanded his attention. He walked, bare-footed into the hallway and picked up the receiver.

"Jack, good morning," It was Red's voice with a tinge of concern. "You didn't call and I thought you might be sick or something. I didn't mean to bother you but I just wanted to be sure everything was ok."

"I'm good, Red. Everything's dandy. Just slept in late, I guess." Jack tried to clear his mind to make plans for the day. Little voices with buzzing questions and chaotic directions were fighting for control inside a still sleepy head. "Must've forgot to set the alarm," he offered as a good excuse.

"Red," he said after a brief pause, "why don't you take out your book and call around for collections today. You know, find out if people can send money in the mail or we need to come round and pick it up. I think I'm gonna stay around here and get our gear ready for the Gruber job. Give yourself a day on the books, you've earned it. Tomorrow we'll go out and plan our work schedule for the next couple of weeks."

"Sure, Jack," Red responded to the surprisingly generous offer. "You sure you're ok?"

"I'm fine! I'm fine! You go on and get us some money in, ya hear?" Jack concluded the conversation by hanging up the phone.

Methodically the old man found himself pouring his usual bowl of cornflakes and munching on a piece of toast while staring out the kitchen window. When the dishes were cleared he went into his bedroom and located the small sandwich bag. The seal was tight and nothing had escaped. Jack poked the plastic container with his finger and watched as the pinkish ooze moved around inside. Finally, he made up his mind.

Pulling on his denim jacket, he prepared to go outside. Before leaving he opened the plastic bag and with the tip of his right pointer finger he gingerly touched the sap. Then, he rubbed his fingertips together spreading the sticky substance onto the ends of each of them. Carefully, he resealed the bag and placed it back in the drawer beneath his jeans.

Jack stepped out the back door. For some reason the social recluse now felt a twinge of apprehension. Even though he was at least a quarter mile away from his nearest neighbor he looked around cautiously, insuring that no other person could see him or follow his actions. He walked around to the great white and tan sycamore that flanked the right side of the house. A year ago, last winter, the taller sycamore had been hit by a bolt of lightning. Jack had known then that it would survive. But several limbs and the top of the tree had been badly scorched and two partially sheered off in the incident. Despite the damage it was a healthy tree and would continue to grow.

"I hope you don't mind bein' my guinea pig," Jack said as he approached the tree. "If'n this stuff can heal anything, I reckon I'd like to see you get somethin' out of it. Now, I promise, this won't hurt a bit."

Jack had his pocketknife out again and used it to carve a "J" into a flat strip of the sheet-like bark at the base of the tree. He wanted to be able to see up close what effects, if any, the serum would have. He knew he wouldn't be doing such a thing if he truly believed that the tree would have had to bear the scar for the rest of its life.

Without hesitation, Jack began rubbing his fingers across the bark, not in the new wound itself, but above it and then around on the other side of the trunk. He was testing his theory. If this stuff was going to heal the tree, it shouldn't matter where it was applied.

When most of it was gone from his fingers he stood back and watched.

Nothing happened. Five minutes went by and still nothing happened. Then ten minutes ticked past. By now Jack had taken up a position some ten feet away, sitting in the cool dew-damp grass, eyes transfixed to the cut in the bark.

A flock of geese migrating north distracted him for what seemed like only a minute or two. The V shaped squadron droned over his house. He listened happily to the honking of the passersby as the aerial sounds echoed off the distant hillsides. The old man breathed in the warming morning air and let out a contented sigh.

Jack was glad he had chosen this spot to settle. The tranquility of the shallow valley had always been a blessing to him. There was no way he could envision himself living in some house-to-house tract of land with cars zooming around day and night, streetlights chasing off the night critters, or somewhere with the whine of jet engines and ambulance sirens breaking the natural stillness of things. He wondered how anyone could live in those conditions.

When his eyes fell again upon the tree he had to rub them with his balled up fists to insure their clarity. The "J" was gone! The salve had worked its magic! Glancing upward into the highest limbs he now saw no sign of the scorching left by the lightning strike. Although the tree was still diminished by the loss of the treetop and the two top-most limbs, if you didn't know what had happened, the damage was invisible. In the eye of the beholder this tree had been made whole once more.

Jack could not be satisfied with this one experiment. Standing up he retreated to the house where he carefully washed both of his hands. This time he walked around to the opposite side of the house and repeated the ceremony of carving the letter "J" with his Barlow blade. Once finished, he replaced it in his pants pocket and addressed the stately sycamore, "I need to know something, tree," he said looking up into its broad branches. "I need to know if I can heal you without the sap from Mrs. Orber's tree. I hope ya don't mind too much but I just need to know."

Jack ran his fingers around the tree trunk just as he had done to the tree on the opposite side of the house. He tried to envision the carved surface closing in upon itself. "Be healed," he chanted softly but in earnest. Finally he withdrew his hands from the bark. He knew it would take some time so he lay back in the soft grass and closed his eyes.

He was hungry when he woke from the short nap he'd taken. It was always a treat to pick a quick lunch or dinner snack from the limbs of a tree... He dreamily wished the fruit trees were bearing but as his mind cleared he realized it was far too early in the season for that.

Jack finally sat upright and eyed the bark in front of him. There, etched, as it had been at least an hour before, was the mark he'd left. He jumped to his feet like a kid late for school!

"Don't ya worry," he said to the tree. "I'll fix ya right up. Hang on, I'll be right back!"

He hurried inside and again retrieved the hidden potion. This time he lightly poked his index finger into the sap and holding it up like a candle, left the baggy propped up against a box of tissues on the dresser top. Deftly he retraced his steps to the wounded tree and this time pushed the sticky digit directly into the carved surface.

The honking of an automobile horn startled him and he jumped three inches into the air and turned with a start. A new silver-blue and white Buick automobile rolled onto the property. It stopped in the driveway that ran down the left side of the house and into the compound behind. Mr. Cornell, a tall thin man, a few years younger than Jack, climbed out and eyed him curiously as he walked across the lawn toward him.

"Hey, Jack. I was in the neighborhood and thought I saw you out here. You're usually out and about. What are you up to anyway?"

Jack quickly moved away from the tree and walked to intercept his unexpected guest. He quickly wiped his fingers on his pant leg again.

"Hey, Neal, I was just checkin' to see if the woodpeckers were doin' any damage this year. You know how it is. They get to puttin' holes in the trees lookin' for bugs and next thing ya know the bugs'll be movin' in to their nice new apartments." He laughed nervously. "Everything's lookin' good though." Jack was thankful that he had done his carving on the backside of the tree.

Jack knew Neal liked to catch him at home when he could. Neal lived with his wife Emma, about a mile down the road. When he'd become bored, being retired from his long-time job at the post office, Neal would get in his car and mechanically drive his old routes hoping to catch someone out doing something in their yard. Neal knew everybody. He knew that when Jack wasn't busy he could be a talker and looked forward to the stories and useful observations the naturalist could provide as a diversion to him on his slow days.

It was Jack's custom to be polite to people when they came to visit, offering lemonade or sun tea and a bit of conversation. Today, however, he was more than uncomfortable and was trying hard not to show it. He wanted to get inside and get Neal away from the scarred tree. At the same time he realized that he had left the sap-filled baggy lying exposed on the top of his dresser across the hall from the kitchen.

"Make yo'self a' home." Jack ushered the visitor into the chair by the woodpile at the back of the house. "Set yourself down and I'll be right back with somethin' ta drink and another chair." Jack's heart was pounding now. He couldn't believe how nervous he was acting. Fortunately, Neal did as he was asked and Jack hurried inside, shutting the door behind him. He moved down the narrow hallway and drew the bedroom door shut with a sigh of relief.

Once back outside Jack found his neighbor was equally distracted. Neal was carefully studying his wristwatch. Jack sat down the kitchen chair he was holding in one hand. At the same time he handed Neal a glass of cold tea that he had been carrying in the other.

"Ya got a pie in the oven?" Jack quipped trying to put a lighter spin on things.

"Naw, it's Emma. I can't leave her for but an hour or so at a time, anymore. She wants me to get out of the house but she's been havin' so much trouble since that last round of chemotherapy that I can't say that it's helped her much. I don't like leavin' her there for any time by herself. Last week she went out back of the house and passed out cold while she was tryin' to hang the laundry. I told her she had no business out there in the first place. She doesn't mind me much these days. Never did, I guess. Anyway, I was just driving around and just saw you out there lookin' over your trees and thought I'd stop and say, 'Howdy'."

"Sorry to hear about your Emma," Jack said sympathetically. She seemed like she was perkin' up about two months ago after that last round, remember?" He had seen the two driving into town together around that same time. Red's mom had since filled him in on the rest of the story.

The conversation lagged as Neal sipped his tea. Then Jack had an idea. "This tea tastes pretty good don't it?" he said in an effort to make it sound special. "I put some of that ground up lemon peal saved back from my lemons last year down in it and let it set before strainin' it off. You suppose Emma'd like a taste? Let me put some in a little mason jar and you can take it home to her and tell her I was hopin' that she'd get to feelin' better. Might cheer her up. Stay put and I'll be right back."

Jack wanted to do something for his neighbor and was now confident that he could. He went straight to the refrigerator and pulled out the pitcher of tea. Quickly he rummaged around in one of the cabinets until he found a half pint canning jar with a rubber seal and wire clip on lid. He filled the jar only half full so Neal would know that this was a treat meant for her alone. Then with a fast glance over his shoulder he took the open bottle and crossed the hall opening the door into the bedroom. It took only a few seconds to penetrate the seal at the top of the baggy, poke in a finger and then stir the substance into the tea. Hastily he resealed the baggy, this time shoving it back into its former hiding place in the dresser.

As he turned around to leave he froze in his tracks. Neal was peering into the room from the kitchen.

"Hey, Jack, I was just puttin' the glass in the sink. Whatya doin' in there?"

Jack's face flushed white with the fear that Neal had seen something. He stammered, "Uh, um, I was tryin' to find a piece of ribbon or somethin to fix a note on the jar," he lied. Jack hated lying. "Didn't come across nothin' so jus' tell her I sent it along will ya?"

Jack pushed the wire clip over the canning jar lid, sealing the container, and handed it to Neal. "Here now, you go straight home and give this to Emma." Neal accepted it without comment and walked with Jack back to his car. "I'll see ya later, maybe when Emma gets to feelin' better we can get in a longer visit. By the way, I'll be down ta Gruber's place doin' some work over the next week or so. If ya pass by would ya keep an eye on things here, make sure nobody's about? I sure would appreciate it."

Neal was happy to do the favor and was soon on his way. When the car was out of sight, Jack walked around to the tattooed tree. The mark, as he had expected, was gone.

Part 5

As the afternoon wore into evening and evening into night Jack was having mixed thoughts about the whole business. He hated secrets, and lying to people. But he was also feeling the wild jubilation of being able to do good things for folks. There was a power in it. Jack was beginning to sense that he alone possessed something truly miraculous. He alone held the magic to change people's lives.

Perhaps he should bottle it. He could mix it with tea or lemonade and sell it by the gallon. But then people would want to know where it came from and what was in it. Again the vision of a landscape barren of trees flashed into his mind. How could such a special thing present to him such an impossible dilemma? Jack concluded that the essence would have to be used sparingly and that he would have to carefully consider what it would be used for or on whom.

Jack did not sleep as well that Tuesday night. In fact, he tossed and turned as he dreamt of a mob of faces encircling him, a sea of outstretched hands reaching out to touch him. "Heal us Jack!" they implored. "Heal us Jack! Heal us Jack! HEAL US!"

Jack woke in a cold sweat. The dim light of dawn outlined the edges of his drawn window shade. For some reason, he was not looking forward to the coming day, at least not as much, as he had the day before. He decided to try to put his thoughts on healing people aside and focus on the business at hand.

Once his cornflakes were polished off, he got cleaned up and dressed. He called Red and arranged to pick him up in a half hour and then started to leave the house. As he was about to exit the back door he stopped, thought for a moment and then turned around.

"No sense in bein' too careful about things," he mumbled to himself. Jack was beginning to become obsessed with the possibility that someone would figure out his secret and try to steal the ointment. He decided to go one step further and disguise or at least better conceal the fluid in the baggy. In the kitchen he came up with another pint jar and filled it half full of dried pinto beans. He then shut himself in his bedroom and in the dim light located the pouch and its contents and stuffed it down into the jar. Carefully, he surrounded it with the

46

beans. With that finished, he crossed the hall, retuning to the kitchen.

As an extra measure of protection he pulled down on an old rusty counterweight that hung from a pulley that was fastened to the ceiling at the far corner of the small kitchen. A section of floor swung up and rested open against the wall. Clutching the jar safely to his chest he turned and slowly descended a steep stepladder leading down into a dank root cellar. The musty space at the bottom was just smaller than the area of the kitchen above. The dirt walls were lined with wooden shelves that housed canned fruits and vegetables. Many of these had been given to Jack by grateful customers. There were also several tiers of mason jars filled with sliced fruits and fruit preserves that Jack had put up himself last season. On the ground were four large lidded apple barrels and some empty gunnysacks that he had used for collecting and storing fruits and potatoes.

Jack removed the lid from one of the apple barrels. There were only a few apples left at the bottom. In the autumn he would fill each to the top and have enough left over to give to the neighbors. He carefully placed the jar at the bottom of the barrel and surrounded it with apples. It wasn't much of a ruse but he was running out of time and needed to get going. As an afterthought, he tossed one of the empty burlap sacks on top of the hidden treasure. He hoped it would serve to bury his secret even deeper.

He started away then stopped again. No, that was too obvious. What was he thinking? He removed the barrel lid, then the sack, and finally plunged his hands through the apples until he found the jar. This time he set the precious object behind several cans of green beans on one of the shelves. That would have to do.

At the top of the stairs once more, he did a quick check to determine if he was still alone. Seeing that he was, Jack closed the trap door and headed out for the truck. He didn't like the jittery feeling that had begun to become a part of having possession of this source of special power. He wanted to leave it far behind him, at least for now.

Jack was sizing up the root system of the trees that would need to be transplanted when the little cell phone clipped onto Jack's belt began its jewelry box chime. It was about 11:30 a.m. Jack unclipped and flipped open the small unit and brought it up to the side of his head.

"That's great, Neal," Red watched as Jack nodded in affirmation instead of talking into the telephone.

Red wondered if it was a new job they might be getting. He listened to the one-sided conversation while hammering some small steaks into the ground marking the width and path of the new extended drive.

"No, nothin' special about the tea. No, it's the same cistern water I've been drawing for nigh on forty years… Look, Neal, it all sounds great, what you're sayin' but I'm in the middle of settin' up for the work at Gruber's old pasture and, well, I'll talk with ya later, okie dokie? Sure Neal, yeah, I'll be in touch. Bye now."

Jack flipped the phone cover shut and returned to his business.

"What's up, boss?" Red's curiosity got the better of him.

"Nothin," Jack countered. "You got the roadway staked out yet?" Jack walked down to Red's position and visually lined up the stakes to see if everything were on track. "Looks good," he noted. "Finish this and we'll break for lunch."

Red smiled and continued his work.

Jack somehow knew what to expect when he arrived back at his place later that afternoon. He was shaking his head as he rolled up to the side of his house in the old beat-up truck. Neal was there and so was his wife Emma. They had been sitting inside of their car; doors open to the warm air, waiting for his arrival. Both practically jumped up and ran to him as he climbed out of his vehicle. Jack threw up his hands, gesturing them to refrain from hugging him. They were all smiles and Emma showed no signs of the condition that had only yesterday ravaged her body.

"How can we ever thank you enough?" Neal started. "What you have done for my Emma!"

Emma had taken Jack's hand and squeezed it with her new found strength. The tears were now flowing steadily from her eyes. "Jack, you don't know what you've done for me! It's all gone! The pain has stopped, you healed me Jack. You healed me!"

Jack was overwhelmed. "Please, please," he begged. "Don't talk like this. I did nothing. It wasn't me…"

Emma threw her arms around his neck. "Bless you Jack," she whispered in his ear. "We'll never forget this." She released him and almost ran back to their car. From the dash she removed the now empty Mason jar that had been shared with her the previous evening and pressed it into his hands. He took it and smiled sheepishly.

Jack looked at both of them. "All things good come from God. He's always given me what I needed, when I needed it most. Sometimes we get more than we need and it's those times we're meant to share what we have. All I had to share with Neal was a glass of cold tea and some words of encouragement. I figured there wouldn't be any harm sharin' some of that same tea with you, Emma. I'm glad that you're feelin' better but please don't make it out on account of anything I've done. Now run along home and let me get my supper."

Jack walked them back over to their car and stood quietly until they had gotten in and driven away. He shook his head and mumbled a soft thank you prayer to his God. He was glad Emma was doing better now but he was also realizing the consequences of his actions. Jack was a loner, a shy man who preferred his solitude. If he were to continue on this course, others would come to thank him or would want to recognize his deeds. He envisioned his privacy dwindling to nothing. He wondered how he could counter this possible scenario.

Jack was now convinced that he had been given the ability to heal those who were sick or in great pain. The discovery of the sticky liquid potion was not made by chance, but had deliberately been given to him to use as he saw fit, he decided. God must've known that he would never be one to take credit for such miracles as he had been given to produce. And surely, if this were talked about openly, the world would consider him a crazy man if he were to relate a tale of three bright lights hovering in the sky, one descending into an old oak tree.

But why, Jack pondered, why Winfield? Was this a chosen place, sacred to the Creator of all things? Did the people here deserve this gift above all others on the planet? Or perhaps this was the beginning of a new age. There were those who believed that there would be a heaven on earth one day. Perhaps this was the start of such a transformation. The seed, so to speak, that once planted would transform the planet.

The old man placed the empty jar into the sink and ran water into it. The water overflowed and ran down the drain. He watched it intently for several seconds before turning off the faucet. In that moment he had a wonderful idea. If everyone in town got healed at the same time it would be difficult at best to determine who or what was behind it. It seemed reasonable. No one would be the wiser.

"I can only do so much," he half pleaded, as he looked intently out over his garden and small orchard.

Late that night Jack drove five miles north of Winfield to the small reservoir that provided the drinking water for all of the town's residents. In the pale yellow light of a waxing half moon he stopped his truck at the chained entrance to the small lake's access road. Cautiously he put his head out of the window and looked around. Fireflies and low flying dragonflies hovered over the levee banks and the smooth surface of the water. It was the only movement he could detect. The musical croaking of the frogs was all he could hear.

Jack eased himself out of the door and carefully made his way around the chained entrance and down to the water's edge. He smiled to himself, reminded of the days when he would have been daring enough to bring along a rod and reel to do some unlicensed fishing. The way he figured it, the air, land,

and waters really belonged to everyone. No one man or company, or state agency could really lay claim to a single square foot. People were just making up those rules as they went along.

Jack chuckled under his breath. That was about as brave as he had ever gotten when it came to breaking the law or even bending it. He wondered if anyone could arrest him for trying to cure the world. And what a notion! If he had enough of the pink syrup could he cure the world?

The would-be healer moved spryly down the gentle, grassy slope that surrounded the lake. At the water's edge he heard the soft squawking of a nest of ducks in the hollow of a clump of tall cattails there and made his way carefully around them. Studying the shoreline he found an area where he could walk without leaving footprints. Concealed by the cattails, Jack crouched low and carefully opened the baggie's seal. He had no way of knowing if this would be enough to have any effect at all but he patiently waited until most of the contents of the container had dripped into the lake. The moonlight seemed a bit brighter as he completed his task.

Like a benevolent old St. Nicholas, Jack finished his late-night deed, turned with a jerk, and quickly, quietly made his way back to his pickup truck. Then, with an elfin smile, he hopped into the cab, softly pulled the door closed, and drove home in silence. This would be as much as he could do without giving away his new-found secret.

When he finally managed to sleep, Jack dreamt again that everyone was watching him. It was dark and all he could make out were thousands of eyes, all focused on him. He started running. The eyes followed. There was no place to be free from the silent stalkers. Running, running, running, he was too afraid to stop, afraid that the eyes would still be fixed upon him. Out of breath with no place to hide, at four thirty in the morning Jack sat bolt upright in bed. A cold sweat covered his body; his wet pajamas clung to his skin. He got up and in the darkness, showered, and then dressed for the day ahead.

In the days that followed Jack wasn't at all certain if he was sleeping or awake. Although he seldom watched TV or listened to the radio, his curiosity got the better of him. The airwaves were electric with the news of hundreds of mysterious "healings." People were checking out of the small community hospital, patients claiming the ailments that brought them there no longer existed.

Several doctors were interviewed with stories of people with critical medical conditions, including the wounds of one man, who had been shot during an argument with his neighbor, being completely cured. No explanation could be found; it was further reported, to elucidate the miracles.

Even Doctor Bowman was interviewed by *The Winfield Daily News*. He deduced that it had to be something in the local water. If it was an airborne pathogen, he said, we would be seeing the results across a wider swath of the county, or perhaps in other areas of the state.

"Smart man," Jack thought as he read the report.

Medical specialists and scores of religious fanatics seemed to come out of the woodwork. The air, the food, and the water were tested for abnormal chemicals but none were to be found. The CDC had set up a makeshift office in the town hall and was interviewing people who were claiming to have been healed.

The theological pundits claimed this to be a sign of God but spent most of their time trying to lay claim to the miracles themselves. Some would state outright that it was through the words of their prayers that these things became manifest. Before the week was out, there was a pilgrimage of thousands of outsiders to the small community. Motor homes lined the sides of the streets. Motels filled and restaurants buzzed with all manner of tales relating to the luck of the town's citizenry. Local churches filled to capacity and overflowed.

Some opportunists would work feverishly to take advantage of the situation, setting up tents for on-the-spot revivals, selling t-shirts proclaiming the year of the Winfield Miracles. Others were selling elixirs that were touted as the one, the true cure-all. FDA officials were all over those guys. It wasn't long before arrests were being made and church leaders and self-acclaimed gurus were at each other's throats over whose God had done the deed.

Despite the disharmony that was beginning to sweep the community, Jack elected to remain silent and go on about his business. The work on the lot continued and he and Red had cleared the extended roadway and relocated most of the smaller trees on Mr. Gruber's property. Jack secretly brought along the baggy, with the remainder of the sticky residue inside. Each day they worked the project, as the small sassafras and elm trees were moved and replanted he lightly swiped the interior of the baggy with a finger and then touched the relocated tree. He knew that the anointment would almost certainly guarantee the survival of his arborous patients.

Nearly two weeks had passed since the midnight run to the reservoir. The baggie was still sticky on the inside but the pink substance was nearly gone. Jack pondered on returning to the tree but decided that it was too risky. So far no one suspected Mrs. Orber's tree as the source of the miracles. Most of the focus was on the water. Interestingly enough, by the time they started testing there were no remaining signs of the healing substance to be detected. And within three days of the midnight event people were drinking the water without the life-changing effect taking place. This was especially true of the outsiders who had begun pouring into the sleepy village. Jack was beginning to feel a little sorry for them.

The following day would change all of that, however.

It started with an odd noise outside of his bedroom window. It was about five o'clock in the morning. Jack lay very still and listened. There were people outside of his home. Not just one, but many. He began hearing cars, engines stopping, and doors slamming. He heard adults and children, even barking dogs. Jack was on his feet and dressing. He dared not turn on the light.

Jack had not replaced the near empty baggy in its cellar hiding place the previous evening. Nothing had tipped him as to

53

this sudden swarming. His heart was pounding like a freight train. As quietly as he could he moved into the kitchen and peered out the curtained window. The back yard was full of people! Jack quickly realized that the house was surrounded. He instinctively reached into his pants pocket and felt for the plastic baggie. There was nowhere to hide it now. He quickly began to panic. Recalling earlier days, getting ready for shore leave in an unfamiliar port of call, he opted to push the flattened baggie down inside his thick woolen sock. It had often been the safest place to keep emergency money. Now he hoped it would be the best place in this new and unusual situation for his new-found treasure. He pulled the cuff of his jeans down over the concealed packet and stood back up straight.

A dark-skinned man wearing a tunic and turban was now pressing his face to the glass window. "There he is! He has awakened! I can see him moving about in the kitchen!" the man shouted to the crowd. Jack backed away from the window not knowing what to do next. He decided to get a feel for what he was up against and took the short hall to the living room. Pulling the shade aside he looked out the window on his front lawn. There were at least a hundred faces staring back at him and another shout went up, "He's up! I saw him!" He saw film crews and vans with transmitter dishes affixed to their roofs. There was no way to escape this tidal wave of humanity.

Jack let the curtain fall back in place. He had never had to deal with so many people before. For a moment he stood frozen in the dim-lit kitchen but by now people were knocking at both doors. He looked out through the window again only to see a sea of faces staring back at him. Then he noticed that many of the watchers were clutching newspapers and waving them in the air. Something was up. Something had caused this gathering on his property.

Jack knew that he did not want to become a prisoner in his own house. He would have to find out what these people knew and figure out a way to get rid of them. Then he saw that some of them were inadvertently trampling his garden. Something snapped and he reacted.

The old man threw open the back door and yelled out to the crowd, "Get away from my garden!" He was waving his hands wildly and pushed into the now surging wall of people. As he attempted to pass through the throng he realized that people were pushing each other, attempting to reach out and touch him. He ignored their actions and continued to make his way to his trampled plants. When he reached the area he turned to face them yelling, "Get outta my garden, you're killing my plants!"

Realizing the boundaries of the tilled and planted dirt people looked sheepishly at the ground and began to move out of the growing space. As he stretched out his hands, forming a humble barrier, Jack watched as the responsive mass now moved around in front of him. The people who had been in the front yard poured around both sides of the small cottage and attempted to position themselves in order to get a glimpse of the shy little man. Cameras snapped pictures and microphone booms hung waiting in the pre-dawn air.

When he spoke again the crowd fell silent. "What do you people want here?" He demanded. "Why have you come into my home like this?"

A lady standing near him held up her copy of *The Winfield Daily News*. Across the front were the headlines: ***Local Couple Names Healer***! Everyone in the yard who had been clutching a copy now held it up. Under the headlines was a picture, his picture. The likeness had been taken by a local reporter during a cleanup effort after a big storm two years ago. Red's mother had called him to say that he and her son had gotten their picture in the paper at the time, but he had not seen it until now.

Jack took the paper from the lady, studied his cropped portrait briefly, then read the first paragraph:

Mr. And Mrs. Neal Cornell revealed today that Jack Harmond, a local resident had given Mrs. Cornell what appeared to be iced tea three weeks ago. As a result of her drinking it, within a short period of time it had miraculously caused her cancer symptoms to disappear. She and her husband

Neal, a former postal carrier in the area, had attempted to thank Jack for the healing but he refused to take credit at the time.

His face paling, Jack handed the paper back. "This is all a big mistake," he heard himself saying. "I had nothing to do with it. The Cornell's are good friends but I had nothing to do with her condition. All of these things are in God's hands. Everything is… Everything that is a part of this earth is a gift from God. If you look hard enough you'll see that miracles happen every day! Now please, please go home and leave me in peace!"

The crowd seemed stunned and fell into an awkward silence. Looking over their heads, Jack now noticed that three men in black suits and sunglasses had taken advantage of his short speech. Without permission they had slipped inside of the house and were now coming out the back door, clutching something covered in an old dishtowel.

"Hey, you there! What d' ya think you're doin'?" Jack pointed to the men coming out of the house. A yard full of eyes now turned on a man dressed in a dark blue suit flanked by two others dressed in similar threads. Someone close to them grabbed the towel and pulled. The man holding it juggled the item like it was a bomb about to explode but recovered it quickly. It was a gallon jar half full of a reddish brown liquid.

Suddenly the crowd was a frenzied mob. In the same instant two shots were fired. One of the men accompanying the man with the jar had a pistol now aimed in the air.

"Stay back!" he shouted. "We are federal agents and we are seizing evidence. This man may be endangering lives with an unsafe substance. It's our job to determine what he has in here!" The second bodyguard now waved to a man waiting in a black sedan. The car's engine fired up and pressed its way through the crowded driveway. When the car was close enough the three men lunged through the crowd and into an open car door. The car's horn blared as it attempted to make a U-turn to exit the property. But by this time the crowd realized the implications of the act. People started yelling and pounding on the hood and roof of the car. The driver ignored the assaults and throwing the vehicle in reverse, continued moving until the vehicle backed out onto the main road. At that point he hit the accelerator and roared off towards the city.

Many of the people who had come looking for the source of the cures now dashed to their cars and frantically attempted to follow the unmarked government vehicle. The TV crews filmed all of the action and then decided that the story would be with the agents. Men and equipment scurried for waiting vehicles. It was a horrific scene with men and women running and yelling, pulling kids and dogs into SUV's and sedans and kicking up a thick yellow dust wheeling and speeding off in hot pursuit. They paid little attention to the fact that they were tearing up chunks of lawn and rolling over hedges and rose bushes. At this point Jack wasn't certain whether to feel relieved or to be sick to his stomach.

But everyone had not left. Forty or fifty people still remained. They gathered themselves together and again began to reach out toward the frail man.

"Heal me. Heal me," the remaining voices began begging in unison. He noted people were moving about on crutches; several were in wheelchairs, two had seeing-eye dogs by their sides, some were dragging along small green tanks of oxygen, others were very old. They pressed closer and closer.

The healer felt helpless now. He could not agree to help these people without risking a never-ending barrage of hopeful pilgrims.

"I'm sorry, I can't," he said as he made his way back towards his back door. "Please, *please*, go home!"

Jack felt like he had been kicked in the stomach when he finally managed to get back inside his house. The place was in shambles, drawers spilled out, cabinets open, even the mattress on his bed had been pulled off of the frame and lay in the center of the small bedroom. The door to the cellar was open. He didn't want to think what he would see if he looked down there. He pulled the trap door down and went to the refrigerator. They hadn't even bothered to close the door. He grabbed a jug of milk out and pushed it shut. From an open cupboard he pulled down his favorite cereal, got a spoon and bowl and sat down at the table. In silence he ate his usual breakfast, knowing full well that he could do nothing to change the circumstances that had led him to this point in his life.

Part 6

Doctor Bowman nodded in sympathy. He was well aware of the ensuing newspaper articles and the commotion that befell the small rural community following the mysterious circumstances surrounding the healings. At the time, he had chosen to ignore much of the hysteria that surrounded the whole affair. Nothing would have pleased him more than reading all about the findings of the federal agents. However, weeks passed without any mention of the curative elixir. In fact, no one had ever offered up what he considered a plausible explanation.

Now, face to face with this elderly gentleman, he was slowly becoming cognizant of the importance of the event as it pertained to this one man's life. The irrational belief that Jack Harmond was somehow selected by his God to change the world could only be construed as psychotic. He made a mental note to convey his beliefs to the doctors in charge of the case.

Jack continued his story unabated.

* * * * *

As he finished his bowl of cornflakes the telephone rang. Hesitantly he decided to answer it. It was Red.

"Jack, have you seen the paper?" the voice sounded like a kid talking to Santa. "They say you're the healer!" There was a pause. Jack tried to think of a response and couldn't. "Who would believe such a thing?" Red continued, trying to be nonchalant about the whole affair.

"I had some people come 'round this mornin'," Jack finally volunteered. "It's no big thing. We've got to get over to the Gruber parcel and take down that pin oak. Are you ready?"

"Well, yeah Jack," Red said, the wind let out of his sails. "Sure, I'll be ready when you get here."

Jack made sure the front and back doors and all of the windows were locked as he headed once again through the steadfast group of followers. They parted like the Red Sea as he strode across the grass heading for the tool shed. Inside he worked silently, knowing that all the while his every move was being watched. Those closest to him extended hopeful hands to touch his shoulder or arm. Every once in a while he would say, "excuse me," as he carried tools, ropes, and the chainsaw to his truck.

"Please go home," he said once more as he climbed into the driver's seat and started the engine. Several people ran for their cars hoping to follow. The rest could be seen sitting down in the back yard.

At Red's place his mother was there to greet him. "You saw the paper, huh, Jack?" Red slipped up and into the cab. He noticed the trail of vehicles that had followed his partner. He had always had a notion that there was something special about this otherwise inconspicuous tree man.

"Pray for me an' the boys, will you, Mr. Harmond?" She reached out and touched the old freckled arm that hung out of the truck's window. Jack could only smile dumbly.

"Aw, Mom," Red leaned forward to see around him. "Let him alone will ya?"

Thankful for the reprieve, Jack carefully made his way around the house's front circle drive and headed back out the way he had come in. The two men were silent at they passed through a stretch of road lined with cars on either side that was nearly half a mile long. In his rearview mirror he could see the havoc of the many drivers jockeying to get turned around and on their trail again. One car made a quick maneuver to get in the lead and was side-swiped by an oncoming van. The whole procession stalled and Jack hid a slight smile of relief.

Before Red could begin the old man pulled his cap down tight on his head as if preparing for a deluge. Then he turned to his coworker and simply said, "It's a mistake, son. There's nothin' special 'bout me. We've got a hard days work ahead of us and we need to see clear to getting' it done."

Red, although disappointed in the downplaying of all of the excitement, knew better than to stir anything else up and sat quietly for the remainder of the trip to Gruber's lot.

Unfortunately, it did not take long before the convoy behind them caught up and a full-blown parade trailed behind the rattling green pickup. Jack sighed when he saw them in his rearview mirror but said nothing as he drove down to the creek and took the gravel drive off to the left and across the small bridge. As he pulled up the gentle grade to park the truck he watched as his followers again took to the shoulders of the road. And then they came. Flush-faced and with hopeful looks the many eyed the two workers as they unloaded their gear.

Jack began to get concerned as the crowd once again drew near. "We'll be cutting a tree down today," he said, trying to sound as loud and official as he could. "This here property is private. Now I don't want to see no one get hurt so you all just turn around and go back the way ya came."

Almost unexpectedly the seekers began talking amongst themselves and as a group they fell back to the edge of the small gurgling brook. Many took advantage of the shade provided by the two surviving willows and sat down to watch and wait.

Now Jack focused on the tree. He knew that Red would have to top it before they could take it down. There was less risk that the strong trunk would splinter as it was felled if he did this. Red was his legs these days. He watched as the boy carefully strapped on the climbing cleats and put on a safety belt to tether him securely once he arrived at the point where he would make the cut. He then threw a long coil of nylon rope over his shoulder.

Meanwhile, Jack busied himself with setting up the ladder at the base of the tree. Once that was done he then got the chainsaw from the back of the truck and placed it on the ground nearby.

When both were prepared Red began the climb. The ladder took him the first ten feet and then he began pulling himself from one branch to the next, ever moving upward. He felt confident as he climbed and quickly decided not to use the rope to haul himself up into the tree. As he passed the thirty-foot mark he looked down. Jack had his eyes on Red the whole way.

"You're doin' fine!" he yelled up. "Watch your step. Use the rope if'n ya need to. That's what it's there for, ya know."

Even as he said the words Red's foot rested on a rather small limb and he heard a faint crackle. Quickly he shifted his weight and moved off of the brittle branch. He looked down and waved, smiling and giving a quick thumbs up signal to show he was alright. He could not help but notice the audience that was now watching the whole affair from the creek's banks. Carefully he proceeded, moving around the trunk as he ascended, like a squirrel fearlessly seeking higher ground. It wasn't long before he reached a point about ten feet below the treetop.

The branch that he now sat on was stout and supported his weight easily. The trunk next to him was just less than a foot in diameter and he carefully turned himself to place his back against it. Now he had to go to work. Although the chainsaw was a light model weighing in at around fifteen pounds he would have to pull it nearly 40 feet up into the tree. Red removed the rope from his shoulder, fastened one end to his belt, threw the remaining coil over a large branch above him, and let the length drop to the ground. When it hit the dirt the old tree master secured the chainsaw to it and waved a signal for him to pull it up.

It seemed to take an eternity to lift the small cutting tool to his perch. Red sweated and grunted as his gloved hands grappled with the nylon rope. The saw seemed to snag on every other branch. The half inch cord was slippery and not easy to hold onto. When it was about halfway up Red stopped pulling. With a good deal of effort he wrapped the chainsaw tethered rope around his right leg to hold it in place while using his freed hands to make a quick half hitch knot, securing the line to itself just above his own perch. This accomplished, the young man was able to let go of the chainsaw for a brief rest.

Red wiped the sweat from his eyes. It was a hot day and Jack was glad that they had gotten an early start. After a moment's pause Red began hauling up the saw, pulling at the rope hand over hand and letting the slack fall back over the branch on which he was sitting.

Finally the chainsaw was in his hands. Red carefully repositioned himself on the limb, now facing the trunk of the tree.

"Set yerself up," Jack called from below.

But Red was visibly distracted. He looked over at the crowd of people and could not resist the urge to wave and once again give his thumbs up sign. Ready to show off his skills, he reached around the right side of the trunk holding the chainsaw up and away from him as he pulled the starter chord and it fired to life.

First he would notch the right side and then he would come around to the left to make the final cut. It was a simple job. He had done it several times on smaller trees. He cut the small wedge from the right side. The chainsaw did its work, easily chewing its way through the bark and into the core of the tree. Red pulled it away and then shifted to the left.

"Look out below!" he cheerily yelled down to his mate on the ground.

The shiny spinning blades made the top cut first. Then the second cut was made.

Jack could not believe his eyes as he saw the last cut being made to the trunk with the rope secured to the branches above Red rather than the one he was sitting on, as should have been done. He let out a fierce, "Noooo!"

The treetop wavered for an instant before snapping and falling over, crashing down through the limbs below. As it fell the unchecked half-hitch knot stayed in place. There was a sudden, tight tugging at Red's belt. Before he realized what was happening the rope snapped taught and the young man's slender body was wrenched off of the safety of its perch. He plunged to the earth.

On the banks of the stream a woman screamed hysterically and children cried out. Stooping over the broken body of his young apprentice Jack yelled out, "Someone call 911! Call 911! Damnit call 911!" Using the cloth of his own shirt he wiped the blood from Red's face, staring horrified at the motionless body. He had nothing to lose and reached into his sock to retrieve the baggie. He didn't care if anyone was watching now. He pulled it open and smeared his fingers on the inner surface. His fingers were sticky with the last bit of residue, and he knew he had the power to heal. It would just be a matter of touching the young man's face. He would see the eyes open, feel the warmth of his breath as he gasped for air and was revived.

It did not happen. The eyes did not open; the heart did not resume its palpitations.

Red was dead. An ambulance arrived ten minutes later in a wail of sirens. Nearly numb to all that was happening, Jack had shoved the baggie back into his pants pocket and wiped his hands on the trunk of the decapitated oak. The emergency medical vehicle left in silence. The tree doctor stared after it, then glared down at his hands and in an uncontrollable rage wiped both on his pant legs and yelled to the crowd, "No more! Do you hear me? No more!"

Jack could barely see from tear-swollen eyes as he rudely pushed past a cluster of followers blocking the door to his house. His entire body shook as he tried to fathom the words he would use to tell Red's mother and brother the dire news.

Inside, hands trembling in a rage he had rarely known, Jack flushed the baggie and its remaining contents down the toilet. He couldn't believe that this mysterious remedy was so useless when he needed it the most. If it were a gift from God why couldn't it go the next step? Why couldn't it give life?

There was an unbelievable aching in Jack's heart, worse than any physical pain he could have imagined. He had loved Red like a father. It was inconceivable that the Creator, He who could bring to this world the magic of healing would, without hesitation, continue to allow mortality to have a hand in the destiny of man. It was senseless. It was unthinkable!

Three days later, at Red's funeral, when Reverend Thompson spoke of the mysteries of God, Jack's fists clenched and tears once again streamed from his eyes. In his shame he spoke to no one and left afterwards in an abject silence.

Despite the tragic event, a small band of believers continued to camp in his front yard and in a half dozen vehicles parked on the far side of the county road. Each day, although fewer and fewer of them remained loyal, some still waited for the next miracle.

The tired and broken old man now refused to leave his house. He heard chanting and singing before he went to bed and before he rose on each seemingly endless day. He wished he had a shotgun so he could chase his followers away but knew deep down in his heart that he could never use it.

A week passed, then another. Some of the faithful began to become concerned for the Healer. Finally, at the urging of a longhaired, beaded nomad, word was taken to the authorities in Winfield and a sheriff's car came out to check on the recluse. They found Jack sitting in the kitchen, staring at an empty box of cornflakes. He was taken to the local hospital, treated for malnourishment and dehydration and then transferred to a nearby mental health facility for observation and treatment.

Part 7

"I've had plenty of time to think here," Jack said calmly, looking into the eyes of the young doctor who now sat, lost

64

deep in his own thoughts. "There were all those people around me who were tortured of sense and soul. I could have made 'em all feel better. I could have! Sometimes I wanted to run out and get some of that syrupy sap and slap it on all of them. I could have taken away their pain. I could have changed so many lives, perhaps thousands, maybe millions. Don't you see it was given to me to do! I was the Miracle Man!" his voice peaked for an instant.

Jack was trying his best not to confuse the doctor with emotional outbursts but the emotions within him had begun to feel unleashed, unrestricted, bubbling to the surface like never before.

"All this time I know'd I couldn't do it again. I figured miracle healing was only meant to be done by saints and angels. I ain't neither of those things. Yeah, you doctors can put on bandages and give out your pills. You even got vaccines to prevent epidemics, but when it comes right down to it, no simple man can change the laws of nature. There's a reason why everything is the way it is. Even the occasional miracle, there's a reason…"

"Could you show me exactly where in the tree…" Richard's face flushed for even having uttered the request out loud.

The man of medicine fell silent. The doctor's mind teetered on a precarious point of consciousness. His palms sweated and deep inside he could feel the power of suggestion inching its way to the core of his being. Jack Harmond's tale had such a ring of truth to it. Could God really exist? Could he have lived his whole life unaware of such a great power?

As if in answer Jack went on, "There's more, Doc. That wasn't all there was to it. No sir, ya see during the second week of the second month that I was sittin' in here I had me a visitor. It happened late one night. You remember we had another big storm? It rained like cats and dogs that night, and the thunder! It was so strange and wonderful that I was really scared for a while there. But I got back the faith that I'd lost, Doc! I got it all back! You see, the miracle is out there, Doc, not in here.

Always was, always will be!" Jack's voice took on a volatility now that was disquieting to the young doctor. Regardless, he decided to hear the finale of the amazing story without comment.

"There was a bright white light and a presence like nothin' I ever seen. It came into my room that very night. A soft voice spoke to me, too. It wasn't just in my head, neither. It was a soft voice," he emphasized. "It comforted me for the loss of my good friend Red and assured me that I was not to blame. Then I was taken to a place high above the earth to look down upon her. I felt as if I was sitting in the palm of someone's hand. I was as alive as I've ever felt before in my whole life. Everything was crystal clear. It was as if I was sittin' at my breakfast table eatin' a bowl of those great cornflakes. Ya know, God really hit it right when he let folks figure out how to make cornflakes. Best food on earth..." Jack's voice faded as he drifted to another place.

Dr. Bowman shuffled to his feet hoping to center a man who was obviously suffering from some form of psychotic break. He had to admit, the old-timer had him going for a while. "What a great story," he thought as he smiled sincerely at Mr. Harmond, wanting to do whatever he could to help.

"The voice spoke again," Jack said in a whisper. "He, that voice, He asked me what I thought about the planet. I wasn't sure what to say. I thought for a moment, then I answered that it was a marvelous thing to look at with the trees, and lakes, animals and such, and of course the people. And I had to say that only the greatest of creators could have had the time and patience to put it all together like what's been done. Then the voice asked me what it was like to live without pain. Did it make life better or worse? I had a hard time answering that one. Finally I said, to be a part of it all you can never stop feelin' things. It comes with the territory, the good and the bad."

Doctor Bowman cleared his throat uneasily. "And what was said to that?" he asked softly, certain now of his patient's unsettled state of mind.

"Well for one thing He said that the time had come to take back the healing spirit from Mrs. Orber's tree," Doctor Bowman's eyes suddenly widened and his mouth dropped open in dismay. "We don't want to see her cut down, if you please." He looked up into the doctor's eyes, expecting an acknowledgement.

"And what else were you told?" Richard mumbled incredulously. He wasn't sure if he should be angry or thankful that he wasn't going to be allowed to get caught up in the fever of the Miracles. A tempest of emotions surged within him.

"The voice said that if I was to wait here for three months, three weeks, and three days that all would be as it was meant to be. And I was told to tell you the story, Doc. Outside this place there are eleven people; I saw them that night in my vision, waiting beyond the gate. They need to hear the story too. I was told that these people would take our words around the world!" He grinned shyly, knowing now that he had become a part of something much bigger than himself.

Richard Bowman wondered how Mr. Harmond could have known about the exact number of people encamped just out of view of the mental health facility, but remained silent.

Jack now concluded his intriguing tale: "Life will be life and in death, for those that choose to believe, there will be no sorrow and no pain," He says to me. "It never hurts to pray for a miracle. And there will be more miracles! People need these signs, now and again; a taste of the honey, so to speak!

"How about it, Doc? What would you do if'n a miracle was handed to you? Do you reckon 'ol Jack was jus' chose ta be the one to plant the seed?" Jack winked at his would be disciple. "I never did ask Him why he picked me. I don't reckon I even thought to ask…"

Dr. Bowman looked down at the floor once more to avoid the searching eyes of the obviously mentally disturbed man. He knew he would be the laughing stock of his peers if he bought into this intricate but obviously delusional fantasy. God was meant for children and old people who could never come to understand the true nature of the world. Besides, God could never be real enough to communicate His will in such a common fashion as this. The story of an old man passed on to an unbeliever; the whole thing was absurd! He stifled a chuckle then turned toward a small computer desk behind him. Pulling a pen from his lab coat pocket he quickly wrote, "Check Orber tree for foreign residue," on a blank note pad, underlined the words, and then flipped it over.

His own emotions now methodically concealed, the physician visually scanned his patient from head to toe once more. He would try his best to determine what Jack Harmond might need to get his life back on track. The old man sat calmly in his chair, smiling. He didn't seem to have a care in the world. In fact, he had the look of a child waiting for a present.

"Mr. Harmond, have you thought any more about the nursing home I mentioned last month?" Dr. Bowman gazed into the old man's eyes sympathetically.

In that same instant an intense explosion of light engulfed the examination room. It completely blinded the doctor who instinctively threw up his hands as a shield to his eyes. When the light was gone so was Jack Harmond.

In the sparsely wooded field just outside the gates of the small institution eleven people had their eyes on the sky. They had been waiting there, patiently, expectantly for the past six months. First one, then the others had seen the blue ball, four, maybe five feet in diameter shining brightly, even in the light of a noonday sun. It came out of the east, passed directly over them and then stopped above the infirmary. As they watched, pointing and shouting, "Look, it's over there now!" it suddenly dropped, disappearing into the roof of the main building of the complex. In an instant it reappeared, hovered for a moment and then jetted back the way it had come.

Dr. Richard Bowman methodically checked himself over. He found himself standing bolt upright beside the examination room stool, unnerved, and thinking that the blinding light had been the incredible arc of a shorted-out light fixture or maybe even a bolt of lightning. At the same time a feeling of peacefulness washed over him like nothing he had ever known before. The old man was gone. On somewhat shaky legs he stood and opened the door. His blurred eyes scanned the empty hallway. His patient was nowhere to be seen.

Richard's right hand dug nervously into the deep pocket of his lab coat. In a moment of clarity he pulled out the small cell phone that had been secluded there. Scanning the speed dial contacts he paused only briefly at the Sheriff's Office number before cursoring back up to Ann Meyer's cell phone listing.

Ann answered after the second ring, "Richard, is that you?"

"Annie, you won't believe what just happened!" Dr. Bowman cleared his throat. He was finding it extremely difficult to talk. He felt tears welling in his eyes. "Annie, I have loved you for such a long time. I've wasted so many years! For so long, I've only seen what was bad about this world, this life, and seldom the good. Now everything has changed! There really are miracles, Ann! Do you hear me? Miracles! All we need to do is open our eyes to them!" Richard Bowman's voice dropped to a whisper. "Annie, love can be a miracle too! What a fool I've been, all these many years!"

The small receiver fell silent for a moment. "Richard, are you ok? Is everything alright?"

There was a tone of apprehension in her voice and Richard spoke quickly to reassure her, "I love you, Ann. Can I pick you up after work? Something wonderful has happened and I want to tell you all about it."

When the conversation ended, Dr. Bowman glanced down at the small desk. The overturned note centered on the smooth, white surface. He grabbed it up and carefully tore it into tiny pieces and tossed it into a shiny metal trash receptacle. It took him a few more minutes to compose himself before he walked into the director's office and reported the disappearance of Jack Harmond. Dutifully, he described the flash of light and the mysterious exit of the crusty old tree doctor. An announcement went out over the PA system and a facility-wide search began.

Richard Bowman knew in his heart what he was going to do next. Amidst the bustle of the search he exited the building. Orderlies were calling out Jack's name as he walked slowly down the driveway and was allowed through the arched entrance by security staff that had already been put on alert. He made his way directly to where the small group of followers stood waiting.

A young bearded man approached Dr. Bowman as he drew closer.

"What news do you bring?" he asked softly, his companions closing in around the two men anxiously.

Richard did not hesitate, "There is a story that must be told," he began. "We, with Jack's blessing, are charged with sharing *this news, this truth*, with everyone we meet." He smiled as they waited for his next words, all eyes wide-open in anticipation. "It is a story," he said with a new tone of reverence, "a story of miracles!"

A Good Day for Anthony

Breathing in the amethyst-purple atmosphere, Anthony arrived at his modest Bay Area domicile, still reminiscing about the Bad Old Days. Father's morning reminder of the great bombs with their mushrooms of death seemed an annoying distraction to his young mind. The ensuing generations of twisted limbs, blinded eyes, and all the other human genetic defects had made Anthony squirm as he listened. He could never truly grasp the horror. He was so grateful that the End Days had already come and gone. Father, a priest of the High Church of the Masses, would always conclude his sermons with the phrase, "But that was then and this is now." Anthony took comfort in these reassuring words.

It was a seventh day, Anthony's favorite manifestation of the sun-go-round. The morning's church meet was behind him now. Soon he would be seeing his true love, Becca. She was seventeen to his eighteen years and would be accompanied by her mother, Momma Tate, or her brother, Ted. Together they would go to one of the many holograph arenas in the city. Tuckers Town Square, being their favorite.

Anthony consumed the red, yellow, and blue capsules that had been dispensed to him, washing each down with a gulp of effervescent water, delightfully tasteless. He sat at a stainless steel breakfast bar and gazed out through the rear glass wall, contemplating the passive rock garden beyond. He was anxious to change clothes and get on with today's agenda. Impatiently he paused the ten minutes considered necessary to digest his lunch. Mother, in her evening gown, perfectly coiffed hair, and high heels looked on approvingly.

"Have a wonderful day son," she quipped as he stood to go to his room.

Sixty-nine minutes later, Anthony entered the bustling recreational hall commonly known as Tucker's Town Square. Becca walked close by his side. Anthony squeezed her small olive-brown hand gently. Her angelic face beamed. Momma

Tate was with them tonight and she gave Anthony an approving nod.

Which playout shall we replicate this evening?" he asked Becca.

"Oh, let's do figure skating in Central Park," she said with a twinkle in her dark brown eyes.

"Figure skating it is, then," Anthony replied, swiping his right wrist under the kiosk scanner at the entertainment hall's entrance. "Momma Tate do you wish to come with us?"

"You two run along," she replied. "I'll wait in the viewing lounge."

With her response, Anthony turned to the audio receptor and said, "Two tickets, please."

A small screen lit up with the transaction, deducting twenty-two credits from his personal account and the entrance door slid open.

The space was dimly lit with a ring of lights around the outer perimeter of the circular ceiling and a corresponding pattern similarly recessed into the floor. The seating had the appearance of an old school observatory but without the central projector. Becca and Anthony took their seats side-by side, leaving a comfortable space between themselves and a group of six schoolers who were already engaged in their group holographic experience.

Anthony removed the plastic wrapped earbuds and viewing goggles that they had picked up at the door and watched as Becca did the same. She smiled and for the millionth time Anthony's heart was aflutter. Once they had donned the gear, Anthony engaged the digital host and picked the ice skating scenario from a long menu of virtual experiences. He settled comfortably back in his seat and moved the blinking cursor over the "run" button.

In a nano-second, he and Becca were transported to Central Park, early twenty-first century. The pair looked at each other with broad smiles as their avatars dressed and made their way onto the ice, adjusting their balance to the slippery surface. They started out in the learners' lane on the outer periphery of the football stadium sized skating rink. The tops of many New York City skyscrapers could be seen over a wall of deciduous trees that encircled the ice. It was night time and great incandescent lights brightened the glossy surface.

Anthony and Becca had been here many times. Once they adjusted to their cortical optics they began moving toward the middle of the great white expanse. Becca's double was cloaked in a light blue downy parka with a flower embroidered pair of jeans. Anthony's duplicate had donned a brown leather pilot's jacket with a thick wool collar for the occasion. His jeans were traditional Levis. She wore brown knit mittens and he, black, fur-lined gloves. Both had selected chocolate chip earmuffs to complete their outfits.

Together they skated hand in hand, raced, or danced to the music reverberating from the rink's state-of-the-arts audio system. Occasionally they would take a break, sharing hot cocoa and talking gleefully about the days to come. They were and always would be inseparable. This love would see them through to old age and beyond, according to the teachings of the church. Infinity was theirs to share.

The perfect day and perfect evening would end with a light kiss goodbye at the door to Becca's house. Momma Tate had gone in first to leave the two to their simple intimacy. Anthony took a cyber taxi back home. It was days like these that made him feel so real, so alive.

The soft hum of white-noise static filled his dreamless sleep. This was the sublime serenity in which he rested peacefully, night after night...

* * * * *

Anthony's AI was created by a team of University of California students in 2017 and was housed in the Department of Electrical Engineering and Computer Sciences building, located in the northeast quadrant of the Berkeley campus, at the intersection of Hearst and LeRoy Avenues. It was one of a handful of structures still standing in the metro San Francisco area that wasn't completely decimated during the Final War.

By a fluke of fate, an array of roof-mounted solar panels continued to generate the required energy that pulsed through the giant mainframe computer system five floors below.

Anthony, however, would always be blissfully unaware that the real world was woefully silent and ever-so-slowly crumbling into dust.

The *Nu You*

Twelve years previous, behavioral neurologist, geneticist, and medical researcher, Dr. Edgar Salazor, had discovered a key genetic marker and an associated enzyme linked to the development of aggressive interpersonal behavior patterns as they pertained to the brain's unique neural chemistry. The breakthrough came during early lab experiments focusing on a new mood stabilizing drug, sk3-nu, aptly nicknamed Nu You.

Neurologically, since the mid twentieth century, aggression had been known to be associated with the fight or flight processing circuitry, particularly activity in the amygdala and prefrontal cortex of the brain. DNA mapping, begun in the 1980's had lead to the discovery of specific genomes and subsequently many of the biological processes controlled by their encrypted codes.

The *Nu You* amalgam, a series of complex neural inhibitors, had first been tested in small doses on mice with minimal side effects over the course of four, two year trials. This screening was used to ferret out the possibility of genetic mutations occurring over more than one generation. Subsequent tests on monkeys had resulted in docile and seemingly well-adjusted behavior in seventeen clinically aggressive chimps that had been treated over the previous four years. The new formula had passed several key hurdles and after nearly fifteen years in development had finally been approved to be tested on a group of twenty human beings.

It should be noted here that this somewhat abbreviated experimental timeline was only allowed after many appeals to the FDA and had only been given an expedited status due to the groundswell of political pressure seeking to alleviate the increasing frequency of violent crimes nationwide.

The pre-screened candidates would include fourteen extremely behaviorally involved adult wards of the state;

individuals with severe cases of diagnosed autism, schizophrenia, manic depression, and Alzheimer's Disease. The study would also include six "normal" subjects. In every case of the clinically diagnosed behaviorally challenged adults, existing medications would be at or near the highest dosage levels with continuing occasional incidents of irritability or aggression.

As the first of the referred and solicited candidates began to come under revue, Doris Granger, the doctor's research assistant and soon-to-be lead nurse attempted to persuade her younger brother Joe, a hot-headed adolescent, to participate in the primary phase of the testing. She told him that he needed to pass himself off as being one of the "normal" test subjects in order to be part of the group. This new medication, she said, would help him to relax and enjoy life for a change.

Joe was eighteen at the time, and was but one guilty verdict away from ending up in a state penitentiary. Driven hard by a merciless father, Joe's rebelliousness had taken the form of truancy, petty theft, vandalism, and more recently included aggravated assault.

The assault occurred during an incident in which he had severely beaten a player from an opposing team following a pushing confrontation during an earlier football game. He had used his own helmet to drive home his unchecked rage, resulting in a ten stitch gash and a concussion for the ambushed opponent.

As a result, Joe had spent two years in the juvenile justice system. Doris, who was ten years older had agreed to take him in following his father's decision to kick him out of his house, two days after he had returned home from the incarceration. His mother, of course, would have nothing to say on the matter.

Having been chosen specifically by Doctor Salazor three months earlier, Doris had been assigned as the head nurse in the initial human testing program. She had felt the doctor's excitement over the real possibility of a long sought after breakthrough in the treatment of aggressive behaviors, and had become equally enthusiastic. She knew that Joe did not represent an extreme case but decided that the low dose trial couldn't hurt. She had read the research and was impressed regarding the relative lack of side-effects and the high percentage of positive outcomes.

Since Doris had married two years before, the two siblings no longer shared the same last name. She put together a file on Joe similar to the others that had been submitted through proper channels and had made sure his name came up in the final pick of candidates.

Joe reluctantly agreed to the drug trial. Already he and Steve, Doris's new husband, had had words. Steve insisted that he go back to school or get a job and get out on his own as soon as possible. Joe thought the "doctor," who was really only a veterinarian, was a jerk and would have been happy to have moved out if he had had any steady income or a place to stay.

Doris told him that the well-financed program would be like a paid vacation. The food would be good, she had said. Everyone would have a private bedroom and there would be plenty of things to occupy the time. She had to continually reassure him that it was nothing like the boys' home he had been sentenced to but that it did mean an earnest commitment of six weeks time.

The twenty test subjects, including Joe, were selected within the following month and subsequently brought together in a private nursing home, contracted for the occasion. The home had been cleared of its previous tenants in the midst of a bankruptcy settlement the previous year. Each subject would have their own comfortably furnished but obviously institutionalized bedroom which included an adjoining private bathroom. It had been a high-end retirement community until the economy went south.

In addition to the sleeping quarters, the facility included a state certified restraint room, with a prepped leather and lambs-wool cuff setup on a hospital gurney, and a crash cart for cardiac emergencies. The main house also included a day room, a cafeteria style dining room, an in-house pharmacy, two nurse's stations, (strategically located at the front and rear of the building), two large meeting rooms, and two private offices.

In addition, there was a second smaller building on the grounds which included a large Jacuzzi, a steam sauna, a modest exercise room, and separate changing rooms for the men and the women. The facility grounds also boasted an outside quarter-mile running track, a double tennis court, and a large, beautifully tended flower garden.

It was autumn by the time everything had been set into motion. The weather had grown seasonably cooler and the sky an unyielding canopy of grey. Joe considered himself lucky to be indoors and some place relatively safe, although he was initially overly guarded concerning interactions with his fellow "inmates."

He was mildly pleased that it was a co-ed arrangement with both men and women present, although most of the participants were several years to many years older than he was. His instincts told him that the level of personal protection would have to be greater considering the mixed population.

In fact, the staff to patient ratio was nearly one to one. Some were cooks, maintenance staff, or grounds keepers, but that still meant more possible allies in the event of trouble, many more than were there at the boys' home. There an adult usually ended up appearing only after any given incident, always resulting in a lingering period of finger pointing, making it one boy's word against another.

The small pink pills were first given, two at a time on the morning of the first day, a Monday. The pill giving ritual was repeated twice again, after lunch and at ten o'clock each night. Participants were encouraged to try to sleep by a subtle extinguishing of key hall and day-room room lights at the stroke of eleven.

Initially Joe and five or six other participants, as they were all duly labeled, were observed to be especially tense or restless during the first week of their stay. They could be seen pacing and eyeing those around them with a not-so-well concealed look of anxiety or mistrust. None of the small group had slept the first or second night at all. As a result, he and two other participants were subsequently selected for a special intensive treatment option set up and run by Doctor Salazor himself.

By day eight, Joe would begin to feel more relaxed but simultaneously he began to experience vivid dreams at night in which he found himself being seduced by fantasy lovers, being treated to decadent parties, being dressed in stylish clothes, fed favorite foods, being given cars, boats, plasma-screen TV's and other computer gear. All of these gifts were being offered by appreciative friends, relatives, and even some former girl friends.

There was one interesting twist however. During each dream sequence, he would only be rewarded after first providing these same individuals with whatever they said they desired. The tasks given were relatively simple yet the rewards were far more than generous by comparison.

In one of the early dreams, Joe was asked by his sister to pick up a gallon of milk at the store on his way home. At the store he bought the milk then bought a lottery scratcher game card with a portion of the remaining change. When he arrived home he gave the milk carton to his sister who then kissed him on the forehead with a "thank you." She then noticed the scratcher in the bottom of the bag and handed it back to him along with a loose quarter also found in the bottom of the bag.

Joe had seen himself scratching off the first three squares on the card and noting clearly that he had won a $5000 lottery prize. The ceiling then seemed to open up with descending balloons and confetti and twenty dollar bills fluttering down and all around him, as though he had been a winning contestant on a TV game show.

He told his sister about it the next day when she came in for work. She seemed pleased that he appeared to have been cheered a bit by this obviously pleasant dream.

Unbeknownst to either of them, the dream was a side effect of a hidden element of the program that the doctor had kept to himself. Doctor Salazor had decided that this trial might also provide an opportune time to test a therapy-based theory of his. He wanted to chart the potentially positive influence of hypnotherapy and visualization techniques, when used in conjunction with the new drugs, to determine if they might prove well-matched in regards to producing quicker positive social outcomes. One member of each subject classification had been selected for the conditioning sessions. Joe had been selected by the good doctor, along with an Alzheimer's patient and an overweight sex offender.

Despite the occasional paranoid/defensive argumentative spats, there were only two significant incidents within the first two weeks. The first would involve a forty year old man named Jerry. Jerry was diagnosed with Asperger syndrome and had long a history of communicating primarily by yelling, (mostly using one or two word phrases), biting himself, and when that failed, frequently resorting to all out aggression, including hitting, biting, and kicking anyone around him at the time.

On the evening of the sixth day he was seen running out of his room in a confused state. He seemed genuinely alarmed. He kept screaming the words, "Where am I? Where am I? Where am I?" until he was finally subdued and sedated.

The doctor, having had to return in the middle of the night, quickly came to the conclusion that he would have to make decisions day by day, even hour by hour, in terms of adjusting doses of previously employed mood enhancing or psychotropic drugs currently used by each of these twenty individuals. Each participant would be significantly different in their absorption of and reaction to the new formula, as well. Doctor Salazor would ultimately decide that it would be best to sleep on his couch for a while, rather than risk being too far away to correctly assess rapidly changing medical and psychological conditions.

The program included six rotating registered nurses covering three eight hour shifts each day. The doctor depended on them for monitoring ongoing patient health, dispensing medications, and dealing with medical emergencies. They had twelve more aides or orderlies working under them and a half-dozen therapists, mostly during the daylight or programming hours. It was up to him and the on-call general practitioner, the grey-haired Doctor Larry Holtz, to oversee patient health and emotional stability.

In the end, Salazor knew that it was he who would be held responsible in the event of a severe injury or death due to an overdose or unexpected drug interaction. He alone would be ultimately responsible for the frequently adjusted medications and their ultimate effects on each individual participant, for better or for worse.

Jerry was only one of twenty examples of what could possibly go wrong. His current primary mood altering drug was Risperidone, first approved for use in 1994. Jerry was taking a substantial dose. The drug had only begun to be used more recently in treating autistic patients with chronic irritability and/or aggression. Jerry had been on the medication for the past three years.

This one drug alone had a long list of documented side effects including: tremors, drowsiness, fatigue, drooling, and weight gain. Risperidone put a person at risk for potentially thousands of harmful metabolic interactions, including causing possible damage to or disruption of the heart, potential problems with blood pressure, elevated blood sugar levels, and possible cancer related implications. In addition to tremors, muscle spasms and restlessness, antipsychotics also frequently resulted in a neural condition known as tardive dyskinesia, permanent and irreversible involuntary movement of the tongue, lip, mouth, arms and legs. Despite a modest to good success rate in treating the aggressive behavioral tendencies, this one drug also had possible links to Parkinson's Disease, diabetes, kidney disease, and liver disease, as well as documented incidents of suicidal ideation.

And this was only one of a whole host of drugs currently being used in reducing similarly challenging behaviors in people with anxiety disorders, depression, schizophrenia, bi-polar conditions, ADHD, Alzheimer's Disease, those having psychotic breaks, and other debilitating mental illnesses. Despite these daunting challenges, new pharmaceutical treatments were coming out at almost the same rate as new mental illness classifications. It was a very competitive field with the potential for huge financial rewards for those developing the latest mind-altering drug.

The pre-diagnosed patients he had accepted were considered dead-end cases with most psychotropic drugs having already been tried and failed or causing more harm than good. These were the hard core, long-term care folks who had been purposefully selected for this drug trial, with hope waiting just over the horizon. Most would come here with more drugs in their systems than one hundred thousand of their "normal" peers. All of his patients would be taking moderate to large doses of antipsychotics, tricyclic antidepressants, serotonin-specific reuptake inhibitors, and opioid antagonists. To sum it up, it was a pharmacological nightmare.

Doctor Salazor called his wife later that evening to tell her everything was fine and to let her know of the importance of his staying close for a while. Fortunately his wife of twenty years had always been understanding and supportive. This was not the researcher's first rodeo, after all! She would deliver a small suitcase with clothes and toiletries the next day.

That same day he would remind himself that the optimal *Nu You* response time for the chimps came in at just under four weeks, the average uptake time expected for these types of medications. He needed to stay on his toes, especially during the next three weeks, maybe longer.

The second incident occurred four days later and involved one of the "normal" subjects who just happened to be getting the placebo. She was a rather thin and boyish looking young lady, a community college student named Sandy, who had agreed to the test for the $1,000 in incentive money. In her restless boredom she had become interested in two men, Rick, a drug-sedated sociopath, and Samuel, another "normal," who would be taking the new drug to help determine its interactive properties on a so-called "non-aggressive population,"

It quickly came to be known that Samuel did not like being called Sammy. In tracking the incident, it was noted that Sandy chose to sit with Rick during lunch that Wednesday afternoon. The unusually quiet man eyed her eagerly and licked his lips in excess during a meal where the two sat opposite to each other across a small table.

There was a longing look in his glassy eyes that the girl considered almost seductive. She viewed him as a well-built, square-jawed exercise nut. Sandy had watched him work out in the gym over the first few days. In truth, however, she was a bit intimidated, noting that some of the doctor's subjects, including Rick, were obviously heavily sedated. She wondered about his history but neither spoke as they ate.

She had also had her eyes on a second member of the group, a youngish-looking African-American man who called himself Samuel. In fact, he was thirty-two years old, somewhere between jobs, and like her and Joe, strapped for cash. He seemed very down to earth though and talked openly of doing big things in the future. He had an outgoing personality and had done well in retail sales, only to be cut time and again by layoffs incurred in the current listless economy. He felt that this was a good way to make a significant contribution to society while earning some much needed cash.

After dinner many had gathered at the TV end of the community space to watch *Wheel of Fortune*. Some of the group had taken to making themselves comfortable for the duration. Several elderly types had settled in to sleep on the plush couches and cushy naugahyde covered chairs.

Samuel was in the day room, too, bored as anyone there. He was about a half hour into putting together a thousand piece jig-saw puzzle on a round game table. He had already pieced together the rectangular outer border and was focused and making headway in placing the red, yellow, and orange leaves in the sugar maples rising above and behind the traditional red barn that was pictured on the cover of the box.

Sandy had sat down across from him and they had begun to converse about her college activities. Samuel admitted that he would like to go to college but that he would have to save up enough money to make it happen. He repeatedly told her that he would never be in debt to anyone, and was most insistent on the point. "There's gotta be a way, though!" he was heard to say.

A few minutes later Rick walked in, dressed in grey sweats, towel over his right shoulder, just returning from another workout, his third for the day. He and Sandy apparently made eye contact as he passed and she had winked flirtatiously. Samuel noticed the non-verbal exchange and smiled up at Rick, initially unaffected by the perceived interaction.

However, that all changed when Rick pulled up another chair and placed it next to Sandy's before sitting down. Samuel, it was observed, exhibited a brief expression of unease or annoyance at the interruption. In the meantime, Rick was clearly heard to have asked Sandy, (while appearing to ignore Samuel altogether), "Who's the ghetto boy?"

Samuel's face flushed at this offensive imperative but apparently he was able to ignore the slam, calmly saying, "My name is Samuel."

Rick smiled, still fully focused on Sandy saying, "Sammy, I like that!"

Samuel repeated his name again in a more insistent tone, and in a sort of off-handed way Rick responded a second time saying, "I know, Sammy, it's cool, it's cool!"

Samuel then became noticeably irritated and with considerably more emphasis, repeated his name yet a third time, this time staring directly at Rick's chiseled face, "Samuel!"

According to the two staff observers assigned to the room, Rick finally looked back at Samuel in a very puzzled way, apparently not understanding his negative reaction and then in some surprise said, "What's the matter with you? You're looking like you want a piece of me. You gonna fight me? You gonna take me on right here and now?"

To everyone's astonishment Samuel lunged across the table, wrecking the puzzle and physically attacking Rick who, in truth, seemed unable to fight back in any sort of organized way. It was all he could do to push himself back in his chair and attempt to get out of Samuel's striking range. Sandy pushed her chair back, as well, and hurriedly retreated from the fracas.

Two burly orderlies grabbed Samuel first, one on each arm and escorted him quickly out of the room. Rick was now standing and with blinking eyes kept repeating, 'What the hell? What the hell?" Two more staffers then took Rick back to his room for a little "quiet time."

Despite repeated attempts to calm Samuel down, in the end they had to physically restrain him. He remained combative even after a healthy dose of Haldol. But, in the end the medical restraint took its toll and Samuel fell into a deep drug-induced sleep. At that point he was transferred to the adjacent padded room for further observation. Within twelve hours though, apparently calm and unaware of any misgivings, they allowed him to return to his own room. He was seen wandering aimlessly later in the day. He had begun humming to himself, although nobody was ever able to determine the name of the tune.

Initially, there was some confusion as to what actually triggered the fight. Dr. Salazor decided to up the dose of Rick's Olanzapine, fearful of possible future altercations. As a result of this one incident Rick now spent the better part of his time sleeping.

Sandy, meanwhile, continued to be perpetually bored, now avoiding most of the slow-shuffling participants. She was surprised that she had not felt any noticeable changes in her own condition, and hoped this would remain unchanged.

The private hypnotherapy sessions wrapped up at the end of the third week with a total of six one-hour sessions per person. Each of the three were hypnotized separately and then made to watch video clips during the hour-long trance. There were various people with digitally blurred faces featured in the images, along with pre-recorded audio "suggestions" calling for a state of relaxation, a feeling of being loved, and speaking of the derived pleasure found in doing the bidding of those who would make up each person's circle of support, especially as it pertained to family members and relevant social and work-related acquaintances. At the end of each session, each man was given a large chunk of dark chocolate which they were encouraged to consume before leaving the room.

This phantom host of "family and friends" asked for small favors and then reacted as if the requests were honored, bestowing lavish complements and gifts in a virtual party atmosphere. Requests consisted of one-step commands such as stand up, sit down, clap your hands, hold both hands up, say, "please" and the like.

A frequent mantra was interjected, "You will find fulfillment in the desires of others. You will find love in doing more for your loved ones. You will know the true feeling of success, when you allow the people you know and trust to guide and protect you in the day to day matters of life."

The third week ghosted by and Joe found himself becoming ever the more narcissistic in his dream view of the world. However, in rare moments he felt that there was some residual unease. Somewhere beyond his ability to describe it, festered a concern that his pleasure continued to be solely derived by the conforming of his actions to the will of others. He could only be happy if he stopped being Joe. But Joe could now see himself as successful, as having a large and well kept house, an exceptionally nice car, and eventually an attractive and loving wife; obtaining each by following closely in his father's footsteps., something that did not feel quite right.

He seemed to enjoy the associated dreams at first, happily relating them to the doctor, his sister, and even to the relative strangers who now made up the body of the new treatment program. His sister watched him closely but was careful not to reveal the true nature of their relationship.

By the onset of the fourth week Joe had begun reliving previous parts of his life in his dreams, pleasing his father at an ever earlier age. He found himself being given opportunity after opportunity to "get it right" and he grew increasingly more comfortable with the idea of becoming an entirely different person.

As week four progressed, signs of normal social behavior begin popping up throughout the group like mushrooms after a summer storm. Impersonal participants began to become more than names, began to become more active in organized group activities and in the ongoing group therapy sessions. Nearly everyone seemed able to successfully follow their carefully scheduled routines, a variety of activities that now included van trips into the nearby community to go shopping, to go to the movies, or to eat at local restaurants. And then there were the Tai Chi lessons, art classes, and tennis matches, weather permitting.

At last everything seemed to be rolling along smoothly. The doctor still looked a bit edgy as the fourth week ended but decided that it was time that he resumed a normal work day schedule. He began once more to commute to his house, some thirty miles away, at the end of each day's formal therapy sessions.

Sandy's situation also took a turn for the better, at least in her view of things. She found herself having a great time manipulating the now pliable study participants. She found that they were becoming easier to talk into doing favors for her, like giving her their portions of preferred desserts, letting her watch her favorite shows on the day room television, and even agreeing to secret sexual rendezvous.

Another one of the six patients diagnosed with Autism, Selena, was seldom responsive to anyone including Sandy. Before her arrival, the forty-seven year-old Hispanic woman had been virtually non-verbal, but with a nasty habit of wailing pathetically when she wanted attention or wanted to be left alone. Often it was hard to say which she was indicating. Her aggression took the form of tearing up anything she laid her hands on. Attempts to stop her often resulted in lengthy physical altercations.

As fate would have it, Selena would also be given the placebo. It was noted that, as had been documented in numerous other behavioral studies, if anyone is provided with the chance to immerse themselves in a predictable and positive social experience this would often results in some level of behavior improvement.

Such was the case for Selena, who watched in wonder at the growing sense of calm in those around her. Despite her limited interpersonal interactions and constant hand-flapping motions, she was observed to be smiling more often, as well as tolerating a great deal more of the positive attention and respect that was being offered up by her reconditioned peers.

As it turned out, Rick would remain heavily sedated for the duration of the six week study. Fearful of further manipulative incidents, Doctor Salazor had made his decision not to decrease the elevated Olanzapine dosage despite his observably compliant mannerisms. As a direct result, Rick's interpersonal interactions decreased accordingly. For the most part he kept to himself, sleeping much of the time. He became more and more unkempt and his exercise regimen had virtually stopped. Staff spent a good deal of time just getting him to stand up and move around. Sandy continued to feel sorry for him but kept her distance just the same.

As the fifth week neared its end Joe had indeed become quite comfortable with the new personality that filled his very being. He understood now why his father wanted him to do the things that he had wanted him to do, to be the man he had always hoped that he'd become. In therapy he talked adamantly about getting out, finishing high school, and pursuing classes in business management and computer science.

His father was not well educated but had always insisted that Joe get top grades in school, as well as fulfilling a personal fantasy or two involving sports and women. Until now, Joe had hated the very thought of doing anything of his father's bidding. Likewise, his father had long since given up on his obstinate son.

Joe had suddenly come to understand how his father had been rejected by his own father, who would eventually desert him and his sickly mother. The overtly bitter and frequently bullying teen, a youth much like him, had gone on to find work as a stock boy in a grocery store, missing many social aspects of his limited high school experience. Eventually he was forced to drop out of school completely, bailing to go to work full time at the age of seventeen.

From the time Joe was born, some six years later, the man had wanted his son to be everything he was and more. He had worked long and hard and had found his way into the garment district. By the time he reached forty-five he had shrewdly acquired two small clothing stores and set up a non-union sweat shop that made belts and purses. The perpetually angry man had considered this to be his empire, a legacy to be passed on to his only son.

Long before Joe had begun the treatment program he had decided that he wanted no part of his father's business, often voicing his feelings in bitter verbal exchanges with the equally belligerent parent. In essence, he wanted nothing to do with the man. Now, however, it was all he could talk about, all he could think about.

Despite the one hundred and eighty degree change in attitude, Doris began to feel uneasy. She wondered if Joe was really being honest about abandoning his own personal dreams and giving himself over to a man she too had learned to avoid. And yet, with the passing of the fifth week she had to admit there was an astounding, yes, almost miraculous transformation in fifteen of the twenty people who were actually becoming normal (observed as calm and compliant), with the help of the experimental drug.

Personalities were being purposefully reshaped, as if elastic in their new chemically altered state. The autistic man who had "gone off" the first week was now sitting comfortably with others and discussing current events, anticipating outings, and conversing easily with anyone who chose to interact with him.

Jerry, now talking in full sentences, had admitted toward the end of the second week that when he began questioning where he was, it had been because he had felt like he had come out of some deep and unwieldy dreamscape. He described the event as if he had been trapped for the better part of forty years behind a transparent but impenetrable wall and then suddenly, that wall simply fell away! Others had similar reactions to their own transformations.

The three who were given the added hypnotherapy, however, were rated in the moderate response category, failing to achieve the optimum response to the treatment. The doctor was admittedly disappointed at first but thought to himself that the behavior programming sessions may have been started too early in the process or else the duration was too short to prove more effective. He would consider writing it in as a key element of future treatment programs. The combination pharmaceutical and hypnotherapeutic procedure would undoubtedly lead to a Nobel Peace Prize, he surreptitiously surmised.

Despite this less-than-perfect prognosis, the trio remained typically upbeat. It was only occasionally that they voiced concerns about the vivid dreams that by this time had begun to include confusing and sometimes disturbing endings, flashes of colored lights that were random and undecipherable, with an occasional associated feeling of panic.

Although the trio talked about these things in group and individual sessions, by and large they did not seem overly concerned themselves, but treated the matter as a simple annoyance, like a buzzing in the ears. When asked what they thought they could do about it, each responded with a similar question, "What do you think I should do?" Whatever response they were given, it was noted, they took to heart and immediately put the suggestions into practice.

On those later occasions where the on-going counseling sessions were deemed private, the doctor had each of the three recall the psychotherapeutic experiences of the earlier secretive sessions. This, all were able to do in some detail, naming foods, prizes, festivities, and faces, projected feelings and other elements of the prompted visualizations. None, he determined, actually recalled that they were in a state of hypnosis, rather seeing these sessions as real-life role playing games, a "truth" that they had been instructed to embrace once hypnotized.

Finally, at the culmination of the program everyone was allowed to return to their homes, which in some cases would be upgraded to semi-independent living programs or less restrictive half-way houses, accordingly. People laughed, cried, shook hands and said their tearful goodbyes.

Sandy, who claimed to have been shy before being inducted into the project, now claimed to have gained some sense of personal power and a general improvement in her overall attitude toward people and life.

Joe had begun telling his sister that it wouldn't take him long to get back on his feet and out of her house. Almost hesitantly, she too began to accept the idea. She knew that Steve was certain to be happy about it, as well. It would, she had to admit, be a huge burden lifted from her shoulders.

The drug itself was given exceptional marks and would soon be submitted to the Food and Drug Administration for initial production approvals. There were still more tests to be conducted but the pharmaceutical company was elated by the early results. Company stock doubled in value overnight.

Joe would no longer be able to determine his own personal progress in relation to the other test subjects, and for the foreseeable future he would only attend group therapy sessions arranged with the local mental health clinic every six to eight weeks. Although it was strictly voluntary, Doctor Salazor had advised it and Joe had set it up without question.

As it turned out, there wasn't enough time for Joe to resume his senior year of high school and get the credits needed to graduate with his fellow classmates but he had taken his guidance counselor's advice and opted for night classes aimed at helping him obtain a G.E.D. certificate. Surprisingly he had managed to focus on his independent studies and to obtain the certificate less than a month after the annual graduation ceremony took place at his old high school.

By summer's end he had enrolled in a local junior college and had bumped into Sandy who was still struggling to get the credits necessary for her Associates Degree in world literature and/or political science, she wasn't sure which.

Sandy turned out to be just over two years older than Joe and took a distant interest, watching him easily pass test after test, quickly surpassing her own unmotivated pace. In talking to him she had also learned that he was concurrently working in his father's garment shops as a new assistant manager.

His father had rewarded him for his change of heart, but only cautiously. Joe had moved back into his parent's home and had become nearly as passive about his father's disregarding silence and/or unfathomable rants as was his Valium muted mother. On his nineteenth birthday, however, the man had surprised his formally wayward son with a Mercedes Benz sports convertible. Sandy's eyes had gone wide in amazement, upon seeing the shiny red car for the first time.

Within days of the event she began to cross paths with the young man more frequently. Subtly, she began her own experiments with Joe, as if he were no more than a lab rat. At first she asked him to do small things, like return her overdue library books, paying any fines she may have accrued. In every instance he complied willingly and without question.

By month's end he was buying her dinners at fancy restaurants, clothing and accessories, and escorting her to night clubs where she told him to sit and wait for her until she was done visiting with her other friends. He did everything she asked of him without question.

Eventually, Joe's father had begun seeing signs of fatigue and what appeared to be absent mindedness in the running of the accessory shop and in the untimely completion of important paperwork. He assumed that this was the old Joe, reverting to his lackadaisical ways. He came down hard and fast, threatening him with cutting off his school funds and even letting the dealership repossess the car on which he was still making payments.

Joe couldn't understand his father's reignited displeasure with him and asked in earnest, "What do you want me to do?" His father related a litany of instructions and let the boy run with it.

However, there would be a ripple effect as Joe now found himself struggling to keep up with his class assignments. Sandy had sunk her claws in deep and was demanding a steady flow of attention, and money. She was well aware of his weakness to suggestion and played it for all it was worth, even insisting that she had, at last, found her one true love.

Joe was elated, feeling as if he were on top of the world. He decided to cut back on his classes, take more time to complete a coveted Bachelor's of Science Degree, while remaining in the top ten percent academically.

Instead of taking five classes, as he had done over the first two semesters, he now only picked up two. Sandy, on the other hand, had been unable to successfully complete either class of the two classes that she had committed to over the previous semester. She didn't seem to care. Her parents were footing the bill, including off campus housing. She spent most of her time partying with friends, drinking wine and popping Oxycodone or Adderall to help her sleep or stay awake. She had managed to keep this lifestyle apart from the shorter and shorter periods of time during which she continued to abuse her one-sided relationship with Joe.

Four months later Joe again seemed to be struggling and once again attracted his father's ever critical attention. This time he was questioned before the ranting began. Once a "girl friend" was introduced into the equation, the old man relented, even chuckling to himself that the kid wasn't a fag after all. He bumped up his salary by ten thousand a year and advised his son to keep her happy lest he should end up getting the all-too-typical "hell from a woman scorned."

"We wouldn't want her to end up like your mom," he said, chuckling at his own twisted humor. Joe thought about the long-suffering, passive ambivalence that had become his mother's persona.

From that moment on, his and Sandy's relationship took a bizarre turn. Joe would do everything just as she wished. And yet at the same time his expectations of her as a friend and a potential lover went from a boil to a low simmer. He saw her the way his father had seen his own mother and then had come to see his own wife, weak and dependent.

When his father told him, six months later, that he should marry the girl before he got her pregnant, he immediately went out, bought a ring, and proposed over dinner at a local sushi bar..

Meanwhile, Sandy was in her prime, enjoying the best of all worlds and taking advantage of every opportunity. Joe had stopped fantasizing about having sex with her, as it had never been offered. However, Sandy was herself, an insecure individual, giving her body to any man asking, in the hopes of finding her one true love. As a result, she had been eagerly used and passed around until her reputation put off any reasonable suitors. She was nearly twenty-three now and considered herself as being "over-the-hill." Still, she knew full well that with Joe she could have her cake and eat it too. In the end, she agreed to his lack-luster marriage proposal.

Once more Joe was elated, believing the world to be his oyster. The proof was in the pearl. Sandy had long since released him as a party partner, and now, following a hasty Justice of the Peace ceremony, had simply taken the reigns of their questionable relationship, focusing more on controlling his steadily increasing salary than paying him any real attention. Joe thought of this as a true sign of trust and a good omen for a lasting partnership. She even let him make love to her when it suited her purpose. What more could he ask for?

Despite yet another small increase in his already seemingly endless work hours and another compensatory salary raise, dictated by a father who claimed to know the true value of a man's worth, his bank account was hardly ever above the hundred dollar account minimum. Although he was paid weekly, this condition never seemed to change. Whenever he questioned Sandy about it, it was an easy out for her to reassure him by flatly saying that she had it all under control.

In the beginning she did manage to pay the note on their modest suburban home, the monthly utilities, a car payment on their second car, her own little silver Toyota, and to set aside money for food, more frequently eating out than cooking anything herself. The credit cards were another matter altogether.

Monthly bills required just over half of his weekly salary, the best Joe could tell. She had already talked him into dropping out of school, saying that the family business was all he really needed to concern himself with, and that his father would be his best teacher. Without argument he had agreed. He was certain that he had become a responsible provider, although this never explained the missing money. First and foremost, Joe was content with the idea that he was living a normal life.

She, on the other hand continued to take more "classes" over time, using the deceit as an excuse to go out and do whatever she wanted to do, whenever she wanted to do it. She took to doing a great deal of shopping with her girl friends, acquiring a huge collection of shoes, hats, and dresses, and meeting a mixed bag of lovers and drinking and drugging buddies. Frequently, she went to so-called art classes, coming home late with her child-like pictures painted with the aid of one too many glasses of red wine. She said she might like to take cooking classes at one point, but ended up hanging out with girl friends and baking pot brownies.

During this same period she decided to give Joe a small allowance and encouraged him to buy frozen TV dinners and sodas for himself, just in case her 'classes" ran late or she forgot to stop at a local fast-food restaurant on her way home. Joe seemed to take it all in stride.

That is, until just over two years had passed since his life altering experience and subsequent dependency on a steady diet of Nu You pills. Sandy had actually bragged to a few of her closest friends about the mind controlling drug, and how it made her life with Joe so tolerable. It was one of Sandy's friends who first tweeted her about the new questions being raised about possible long-term negative side effects of the experimental medication.

Apparently, a competitive pharmaceutical company had caught wind of an in-house memo noting that after three and a half years of prolonged use, three of the seventen medicated monkeys had suddenly and without explanation become agitated, confused, and by all accounts homicidal. The report revealed that each chimp's cage mate was found pummeled to death by fisted hand or food dish. The incidents happened within weeks of each other, according to the report leaked to the press.

In the article, which Sandy quickly found on-line and read in its entirety, it was further noted that within a week of the killing incidents, the isolated chimps had became morose and despondent. Eventually, she read, they refused to eat or drink. Several attempts to provide motivation through special treats and nutrition-enriched sugar water failed. All three of the monkeys died within a two month period.

As she finished reading the article Sandy felt as if the wind had been knocked out of her. The idea that her own husband could go ballistic on her at any moment sent shivers up and down her spine. She began to panic, realizing all too well that her world was about to come unraveled. She said nothing to Joe about the article. Instead she Googled Doctor Salazor, who she found was now practicing private psychiatry in Maryland.

Of course he could not get directly involved, he told her in a brief phone conversation, but Joe could talk to his local psychiatrist and if he wished, and under clinical supervision, be weaned off of the drug.

Doctor Salazor was careful not to mention anything more about the potentially life-threatening chemical concoction or the covert behavior management program that he had developed for the three now-deceased young chimps and had carried over in the human trials.

The conversation was curt and to the point. He would not tell her about two other "normal" participants and the five previously-diagnosed patients who had had psychotic breaks when attempting to discontinue their use of the drug. One had committed suicide. He would not tell her how the original chimpanzee "programming" sessions had included videos clips of docile primate gatherings, with their digitally blurred faces associated with large piles of succulent fruits and preferred activities. He would keep to himself the secret one hour sessions that were held two nights a week, for the first six months of the mandated five year study. And he would never admit that he had decided to include the unapproved experimentation during the first human trials.

Frozen between having to give up an endless meal ticket and the idea of being bludgeoned to death in her sleep, Sandy got very little sleep over the next few days. It was with a sudden shudder one afternoon that she realized, in her own insomnia induced haze, she had recounted a brief snippet of a conversation that morning, with Joe saying that he had begun having the old dreams again, with the colliding colors and feelings of anxiety.

Besides his own myopic father and quietly vegetating mother Sandy was the only one who really interacted with Joe. Having adopted his father's severe managerial attitude at work, Joe had no friends. Through Sandy's skillful manipulations he did not associate with any of her friends, either. In the end, there was no one other than herself who truly knew his state of mind or regarded it as having any significant importance.

The next day she went out to purchase a pistol. She had told the salesman at a Wal-Mart two cities away that she had heard of several recent robberies and that her husband had suggested the purchase since he often worked nights, leaving her alone in the house. She said she hadn't found one that she liked in local stores and decided to check here while she was in the city on business. She then pointed to the first pistol she saw and said, "I'll take this one."

She was told that she would have to wait a full week before a background check could be done as was required by law. She would have to return in one week to pick up the gun.

Her emotional state began to unravel as she sat up night after night watching her husband toss and turn, dealing with his own nocturnal demons. She took her "sleeping pills" during the day in an attempt to get some much needed rest. Too often she would awaken with a start, not knowing where she was or what day of the week it was. She had gone so far as to alarm one of her best friends by calling her at three o'clock in the morning and begging her to come over to watch her husband sleep, in case she should accidentally fall asleep herself. The unsettling voice that rose from some unknown place within her own trembling body washed over the phone as an eerie whisper mixed with a sort of child-like whimper.

Her friend said, "Get some sleep honey and call me back in the morning."

Joe found her asleep on the bathroom floor when he awoke the following day. He stood looking down at her, at first fearing that she had had a stroke or heart attack and might be dead. But then he saw the familiar rise and fall of her breasts beneath the top of her thick flannel pajamas and taking a deep breath, knelt down and shook her shoulder.

Sandy gave out a surprised little gasp as her eyes opened, seeing his pensive face so close to hers. But upon looking around she said she had forgotten where she was. With a great deal of effort, she managed to get up and make her way back to the bedroom where she climbed into bed with his urging.

Joe tried to fuss over her before he left for work but she waved him away saying she had gotten sick in the middle of the night, she thought she was going to vomit so she had gone into the bathroom and laid down for just a moment, immediately falling asleep. She was fine now, she assured him, and he should go to work.

Just before noon Sandy got a call from her worried friend. Still in a fog Sandy said, "I can't take it any more! I've got to go pick up my gun!"

Her friend asked, "Gun?" but the phone clicked dead as Sandy turned it off in her hurried attempt to discontinue the potentially incriminating call. What was she thinking?

Sandy was awake now, but shaky and not at all sure if she could make the four hour drive necessary to pick up the gun and return home. But it was now or never. She dug into her nightstand drawer found and then popped a couple of Ritalin into her mouth. Then she rose to wash them down with water from the bathroom tap. With every ounce of energy she could muster she reached deep for resolve, managing to throw on a house dress and some flip-flops and then surprisingly, she found herself on the road and heading for the distant store.

The drive seemed endless and it took all of her will to keep the Toyota on the right side of the road and between the blurring white lines. When she finally arrived she parked a considerable distance from the main entrance to take a parking space that was isolated and free from the possibility of an accidental run in with another would-be shopper's parked vehicle. The ground felt uneven as she walked with but three objectives in her addled mind, getting in, paying for the gun and a box of ammunition, and getting out.

Inside she found a lady attendant in the nearly deserted sporting goods section. She seemed to take forever in locating the licensing paperwork and finally asked to look at Sandy's driver's license to take down necessary identifying information.. Sandy handed the clerk her driver's license,   pulled her sunglasses down just enough to reveal the color of her bloodshot eyes, then pushed them back up with a middle finger and a half-smile.

"Cash or credit?" the short, chubby, young woman asked, handing the license back to her. She was looking Sandy over now. A look of distaste flitted across her pimpled face as she peered warily at the rumpled women she seemed to be seeing for the first time. She watched as Sandy returned the ID to her wallet and then began to rummage through her purse, in a sudden, desperate attempt to find something that didn't seem to be there. The plump girl waited with her hand still outstretched.

Sandy's mind was now racing furiously. Where had she put the cash?" She was sure she had taken cash out of the bank last week, or was that what she had planned to do but had never actually gotten around to doing? She began to panic. The ever patient cashier watched as Sandy suddenly stopped searching and stood frozen in thought.

"Damn, damn, damn!" Sandy thought in a whirling haze, hopeful that this voice was only in her head. Sheepishly she looked at the attendant who stood unmoved in her harlequin-like pose.

"It was supposed to be paid in cash!" Her mind shifted into hyperdrive. "Wasn't that supposed to make the purchase untraceable? She would want to tell the police that it was an old gun that her husband had kept in his desk drawer for emergencies, oh these many years. But if I leave and come back with a fistful of cash is this lady going to think it strange, strange that a sleepwalking housewife living two cities away had opted not to use her all too convenient credit card for this potentially lethal purchase?"

Sandy could feel herself teetering and made a waving gesture with her hand, dismissing her own awkward delay and pulling out her bank card. She prayed that there would be enough money in the account to cover the purchase.

The clerk grabbed it from her fingertips, as if she were about to lose a fish on a line and swiped it through the card reader. An hour seemed to pass before the lady smiled and handed the card back to her, wrapped in the receipt. Sandy grabbed it and the yellow plastic bag containing the thirty-eight caliber pistol and a box of hollow-point rounds and headed doggedly for the front door.

By the time she got back to the car she was shaking from head to toe as if she had just been thawed from some arctic glacier. It was after two and her stomach ached with hunger but she decided that she needed to be at home before Joe arrived at his unbelievably dependable time of five forty-five p.m. on the dot. She dug a single Adderall from the bottom of her purse, choked it down, and started up the engine. For a full minute she endured wave after wave of nausea. When it finally receded she pulled out of the parking lot and headed back out and onto the nearby freeway on-ramp.

She would be waiting, she thought as she robotically made her way home. The loaded gun would be waiting, tucked behind a couple of books in the bookcase that he had seldom, if ever, disturbed.

She had already, very carefully, thought this part out. Her husband would enter through the front door, and then as was his habit, go to his small office and check his email before coming out again to ask what was for dinner. She would follow him into the small workspace furnished with its small writing desk, conspicuously overrun by an ancient desktop computer, and the dusty little bookshelf just below a large framed poster.

Sandy had decided that this room would be easier to clean up than the others. The smaller carpet could be replaced if it were absolutely necessary. She would tell the police that he had kept the revolver in the bottom drawer of his desk.

Then she would order him, no, she would command him, like the dog she had always known him to be, to beat her, to strike her across the face. If he needed more provocation she would gladly provide it. She thought about Samuel for the first time in years. She would egg Joe on, certain she could bear the bruising.

At that point books would be knocked aside and the gun would appear. She would tell him to stop hitting her. He would comply. She would tell the police that she had wrestled the pistol out of his crazed and shaking hands and only as a threat had she pointed it at him, pleading for him to stop his uncontrollable assault. It would be a case of self-defense; open and shut.

It was a good plan, she thought, as she reached the maze-like streets of the bland subdivision that looked like so many other three-bedroom, two and a half bath, brick townhouse suburban tracts. She would tell her lawyer about the article that she had found, but only after-the-fact, as if she had just happened to see it after her horrific experience. It would explain everything. She would tell all about his, (not her), drug trial exposure and the ticking time-bomb medication he had continued taking under his current doctor's supervision. She would also mention the juvenile assault charges that she had become privy to in one of the therapy sessions at the clinic.

101

Once the experimental trial had ended, each of the participants had been given the option to discontinue the drug or to continue taking it as a part of a long-term study. With Doris's encouragement Joe had opted to continue. He had seen no reason not to and that had been a pivotal decision.

There might also be a law suit involved. She could file malpractice suits against Dr. Salazor and the reprehensible pharmaceutical company, as well. She smiled to herself, pleased with her methodical assessment of the situation.

Suddenly she realized that she was humming, humming like Samuel had in the aftermath of his brief skirmish. She needed to settle herself. Humming was not her norm. She began reminiscing again about the treatment center and all of those strange people. She shook her head as if trying to wake herself from an unsettling dream. They had taught her something there. It had been a useful experience. She had learned to identify the sleep walkers, the invisible people.

And they had also taught her a stress release trick called visualization. She would need to be calm enough to pull this off. If she played her cards right she might even manipulate Joe's old man into providing her with a comfortable allowance while waiting for the settlement. She needed to be as steady as a rock.

Without even realizing it, Sandy found herself in her own driveway once again. Clutching the yellow plastic bag tightly in both hands, she made her way inside, and finally found herself in the abbreviated office space.

She took the gun out of the bag, found the lever to release the six-round cylinder and loaded the weapon. Once that was complete she pushed the partially empty cartridge box into the bottom desk drawer, shoving it towards the back and covered it with an empty file folder. She used the plastic bag to line the small wastebasket. She then positioned the gun behind a few of the smaller paperbacks on the second shelf of the little bookcase, carefully pushing them up against the cold blue steel. She checked her watch. It was nearly five twenty-five.

She continued to hum softly to herself as she turned to study the lone picture on the wall. It hung prominently, directly across from the tiny desk. It was a travel agency poster featuring Rio de Janeiro. It included bikini-clad women on a white sandy beach, costumed revelers at Carnival, and, of course, the iconic statue of Christ overlooking the city. For a brief moment she stood unmoving. Then slowly she sat down in the cheap desk chair that creaked as it bore her weight. Her hands were visibly shaking again.

She needed to collect herself, calm herself down. She focused on the picture on the adjacent wall and then closed her eyes, visualizing the picture, forcing herself to imagine being in a faraway country. She threw in a bronzed young waiter and a tall mixed drink festooned with a miniature parasol, for good measure. As her breath steadied she opened her eyes, focusing now only on the cool tropical colors that blurred into the wall before her eyes.

Then she almost screamed out loud as she heard the front door swing open. Joe was home ten minutes early!

With blood shot eyes and lips drawn in a tight straight line across her tawny face, Sandy rose and quickly darted down the hall and into the back bedroom where she would wait in dead silence until her husband entered the small office and turned on his desk top computer.

Joe was tired. He had felt himself becoming uncomfortably restless earlier in the day. He could not say why. He kept thinking of flashing colors and a conflicted feeling deep within his gut. He knew that no one really paid any attention to his comings and goings. No one would notice if he left ten minutes early to go home, or to go out an rob a bank for all that matter. Nobody cared, not even his father. He thought about Sandy, sick and undoubtedly sleeping in the adjacent bedroom. He would check on her as soon as he was finished.

As the desktop buzzed to life he looked over at the large, handsomely framed picture. Joe had acquired and framed it, on a rare impulse buy shortly after they had bought the new house and he had claimed this room as his home office.

As he studied the image of that far away land, he found himself actually recalling details of the day on which it had been purchased. On that otherwise unremarkable Saturday he had assured himself that some day, maybe, just maybe, he would be able to retire. This would be the ultimate reward for dedicating a lifetime to those around him.

Joe's right hand began to tremble uncontrollably. He stared down at it, confused. When he looked up again he resumed the surreal remembrance.

One day, he had thought, after his father and his wife, after everyone else had finally gotten what they wanted out of him, he would once again see the balloons and confetti falling from the ceiling. Perhaps he would actually take a trip to see the lights in Rio de Janeiro. There would certainly be some reward for a lifetime of good behavior.

A searing pain suddenly crackled like lightning behind his eyes. Unconsciously, his twitching hand reached for a heavy metal stapler atop the small writing desk. His teeth were grinding and he felt a wave of unexpected rage welling up inside. At the same moment, Sandy appeared at the door. Her glazed eyes fixed o his.

"Hello darling," she said. "How was your day?"

The Galactic Miner

I am too dumb to know much of this,
Here, in this vessel's hold,
Bulkheads black with a rusty tinge,
And the musty smell of bilge and mold.

I huddle in the steamy midst of a hundred mumbling men,
Though, none of us know exactly where we are,
Without lifting a finger to press a button or flip a switch,

We have made the stars!

Snorting and stomping, hooves to the ground,
Bulls before the matador.
Doin' the dance, dodging the dump trucks,
We run with the dozers, gore deep with our horns.

Red flags and dynamite, sledge hammers and picks,
The tools of our journey, our stock and our trade.
Strength and instinct, glory and grit,
Like onions we peel all the layers away.
We dig,
And dig,
And dig,
And dig,
All day,
Every day…

As it was in the beginning, from our training years
In the tubes on Mars,
We have known no other way. And they tell us
We are like the gods…

We have made the stars!

Digging down, down, deeper still,
We strip the gas, the liquid, the minerals we pick.
From craters, mountains, vast airless tracts,
We rip our treasures from the defenseless ground,
To fill the belly of our ships.

Time and time again, we load the goods
Then watch them slowly float away.
And when there's nothing left to take,
They take us to another place.

And say, "Today... You have made the stars!"

Another moon, another rock,
Another "useful" world to maim.
We leave our scars, we leave our flags
We mark the turf where Mother Earth Incorporated
Has staked another claim.

We buzz like insects, to and fro,
We flit across our galaxy,
Removing every resource, securing every morsel,
Every crumb and every seed.

We brag with pride, those still alive,
That we can live on the barest of necessities,
Bread, beer, the occasional breeder,
And, of course, the blessed chance to sleep.
Oh life!
Oh, glorious agony!

We have made the stars!

Yes, I am a company miner
And every miner has his rights.
I have the right to serve the queen. I have the right
To serve the hive. and in return, I will be given

Only that which I must have,
Only that which I must have,
In order to survive.

And by the Stars, I am alive!

I count my age with tally marks
The times that I have shaken me awake.
I figure, twelve thousand seven hundred
And seventy-five, more or less, give or take.
And though I know some time's been lost
In the crunch of double digit shifts,
It makes little difference down in the mines
Where digging deep is all there is.

Don't ever tell us where we are…
Just tell us we have made the stars!

I have toiled in the glow of Neptune's moons.
I've jack-hammered through mountains of stone.
I've been pushed down
Into a thousand treacherous tunnels.
I've worked platforms that bored into boiling oceans.

I've labored in the mines of a dozen dead planets.
I've stumbled through desert and vine,
There's a sameness to every Off-world horizon,
With a drill bit or pick gripped in my hands,
Or a green viper lizard on the point of my knife.

And yet, I bear no resentment, no bitter remorse.
I have done so many incredible things,
And I have gone where no man has gone before!
As if otherwise, I could ever have seen such things!

Yes, I hear this glorious song each day
In the company stores and the bars,

"Thank you, thank you, thank you brothers,
You have made the stars!"

I know that life is a sleepless dream,
A birthright of trouble and tears.
It is the essence of each new experience,
The chance to touch, to smell, to taste, to hear,
To see with my own eyes:

The color of Europa's sky,
The fish that swim through solid stone,
Beasts that burrow in ice and snow,
And all the things that thrive in caves,
The place that humans once called home.

I've seen jungles, wild, with purple trees,
House pods, like piñatas that swing in the breeze.
I've seen flowers that burst into Bright yellow clouds,
Their sickly-sweet smell drives the Dragon-birds wild!

I've looked upon aliens who knew more than most men
About the universe, math, and other such things.
They swim in the shallows of a blue algae pond,
Talk with their minds, sing us their songs.

I've seen ruby red lakes and great silver cities.
I've seen the giants on Hermippe prime.
I've seen sky trains, and hell-cats, humans in zoos,
And carnivals on Ganymede, Ariel, and Titan.

And for every light, there is, of course, the opposite,
All those things that men fear most…
Like hungry Drekkars that lurk in the dark,
A Plutonian ship wreck, Intergalactic War,
The space suit that fatally tears on a snag,
A poisoned quill in the side of your boot,
The chaos that comes with electrical storms.

The green viper lizards of Area 4.
The terrible rumble of tumbling rocks,
That final moment, when you know…
You know too late,
That Death has come and breath will stop.

I serve the master, I have no choice.
I dig my living. This is my voice.
My DNA is registered, check the Bar-code that is
Tattooed on my arm.

I can't tell you what my name is,

But I have made the stars!

Now, once again, my day is done,
I'll fall into a fat and lazy sleep.
A swirl of gasses, ice, and bits of stone
Spin in orbit around my heavy head.
I am a Class III Worker Clone,
I know that I will dream, I will dream the dream
That I have always dreamed,
It is The Way of It:

There are doors that I have yet to open.
There are colors I have yet to see.
There are wonders I cannot imagine.
And I have made the stars today!
I have made the stars!

Tomorrow I will do something…
I will do …

Something new!

Something from Nothing

Tom Delachaise was thirty-four years old. He lived a quiet life in his childhood home, on LaBarre Street in Jefferson, just outside the New Orleans city limits. The native Louisianan continued to inhabit the small house despite the haunting memory of a father struck down by a massive heart attack in the back yard ten years ago and a mother taken by a rare form of lymphoma just this past spring.

Tom was not married and had no children of his own. His job was a routine nine to five stent as a bookkeeper for the regional office of a national chain of what were commonly referred to as box stores.

He was studying online to acquire a Certified Public Accountant license. Everything seemed under control. In his mind, life, as dreary as it was, was all it could ever be.

His lady friend, Sally, was brash and self-centered. She obviously tolerated him for drawing a steady paycheck and having his own house and car. He tolerated her for giving the outside world the illusion that he could love or be loved by a female human being.

Years of childhood and adolescent teasing by classmates who only lived to pick on the fat kid, had exacted its toll on his fragile psyche. With little or no attention from the opposite sex during his formative years, Tom found himself constantly defending his own masculinity, not only to others, but as much to himself, thus, the need for Sally and her dominating ways.

For her part, Sally was never hesitant in saying she could do better. She had said as much a dozen or more times over the three years of their poorly-defined relationship. This was fine with Tom. The subject of marriage seldom came up. When it did, it was almost always coupled with a copious amount of pre-conditions from the would-be wife, including a bigger house, a newer car, and a well-padded bank account. This version of the American Dream was to be her means to finally quit her stupid job as a Walmart cashier and become a "regular housewife." All of those pre-conditions, of course, had to happen "first."

Sally was thirty, five foot, two inches tall, and weighed in at around one hundred and twenty pounds. She had shoulder-length dishwater-blond hair which she almost always swept up into a bun with a short knitting needle-type of skewer to keep it in place. She was cute but often countered her attractive traits with a dour scowl that she continuously blamed on a world that never gave her a break.

Truth to be told, she still lived with her parents and had no real ambitions beyond her present job. Accordingly, she came over to Tom's house two or three nights a week to share microwave dinners, large quantities of diet coke, and an evening of her favorite night time TV shows. They made out on the couch whenever she was in the mood and she seldom stayed over night, unless she was feuding with her mother over one thing or another. Again, this arrangement was satisfactory with Tom, who would, on occasion, take her out to dinner and a movie, just to "see and be seen," as he put it.

It was a Monday. Sally never came over on a Monday. Tom slogged in the front door of his two-bedroom suburban house. His shoulders ached, reminding him that he was just at the beginning of another long and tedious work week. His jet-black cat, Rachel, greeted him at the door. Tom groaned to himself, knowing that this was the day he needed to clean the kitty litter box and that her soft purring would soon erupt into an insistent demand for food.

Tom bent over to pet his only honest companion and winced as he straightened back up. He would need to apply some icy-hot ointment to his lower back tonight. First, food for the cat, then the litter box, then his dinner, some TV time, a shower and finally he would be able to commence the self-administered back rub. Sleep would come soon afterwards. It was always easy for Tom to fall asleep. At this point in life, it was his favorite pastime.

Tom's house was a cookie-cutter version of twenty-nine others in the suburban neighborhood he had grown up in. The living room was separated from the kitchen by a dividing counter that doubled as a meal prep surface and a table with two high bar stools on the kitchen side. A pile of bills and advertising fliers occupied a front corner. He tossed another invitation to get free information about hearing aids on top of the ever-growing stack. He needed to thin it out.

A pale green couch was backed up to the counter on the living room side of the divider. This faced the front wall where a window had been removed to make a continuous surface for an entertainment system flanked by two free-standing stereo speakers, separated by a 50 inch flat screen smart TV.

Additional components, including an am/fm radio receiver, wifi router and a high end turntable which, along with a dozen vinyl records and twice as many cd's, cluttered a small, two-shelf stereo cabinet below the wall-mounted screen. This was Tom's other world.

Twenty feet in, and to the left of the front door, was an arched egress to a short hallway. Inside and to the left was the door to the master bedroom, a space that shared half of the width of the front of the house. Across from the archway, a door to a second bedroom, a narrower space that stretched from the middle to the back of the house. A third door at the end of the hall led to a bathroom that was squeezed in between the kitchen and the smaller bedroom at the back.

His hot water heater and a washer and dryer were in the small garage behind the house. He had come to the conclusion that this was an annoying inconvenience perpetrated by the designers of this subdivision, probably for the sadistic gratification of some band of plumbers plying their trade in the 1960's. Especially during the winter months it would often seem like it took at least five minutes to get hot water to the shower. What were they thinking?

Tom made his way into the kitchen, sink and refrigerator to the right, stove on the back wall flanked by a back door on the left and floor-to-ceiling cabinets on the right. He went to the bottom shelf of the cabinets and pulled out a small bag of dry cat food. Rachel watched attentively. With a pat of her head and a stroke of her back, Tom poured the food into her empty dish.

"There you go, puss puss," he said softly, returning the bag to its designated storage space, then he turned, picked up her water dish, filled it at the sink and plopped it down beside the contentedly eating feline.

Tom decided to open the back door, allowing for a cool evening breeze to air out the house. It was autumn in the southland, and for a few brief hours each day it was less than 90 degrees in the shade. The windowed door, coupled with a secondary screen door, led out to a small back yard which received little attention save being mowed as was needed.

A short flagstone walkway made its way to a side entrance of a garage that had been erected on the right back corner of the lot. Tom had considered building a second story on the garage and renting it out to augment his income. Then he decided there was too much work involved in obtaining the proper city permits and too much money in just getting the damn things approved and signed. The garage itself was little more than a 20 by 40 foot storage shed, and had been as long as he could remember.

From a shelf beneath the kitchen side of the center counter, Tom shook out a plastic grocery bag from a pile and headed into the back bedroom. This area was a designated work space although Tom seldom, if ever, brought his work home. Inside was a small, two-drawer desk and a money-spent-wisely, ergonomically padded and adjustable office chair, facing the doorway from across the room. Tightly packed floor-to-ceiling bookcases lined the better part of two full walls. A walk-in closet spanned the third. On the desk was his father's Dell desktop. It was nothing fancy, but gave him access to the Internet, and more importantly his C.P.A. classes.

He picked up a scoop from a small pail at the back of the room and proceeded to strain cat poop from the adjacent box, dumping it into the plastic bag. Having finished, he added new litter, tied the ends of the bag shut and made his way out the back to the wheeled garbage bin just to the right of the screen door. The cool evening air felt good. He paused for a brief moment to let it wash over him.

As Tom turned to reenter the house he thought he heard a strange sound emanating from the garage. It was not unusual for the squirrels in the area to jump from the large pecan trees at the back of the lot onto the flat garage roof to scout for fallen nuts. Tom listened for a moment longer, and then not hearing anything unusual, went back inside to prepare his own dinner.

Tom peered inside his well stocked freezer. This model gave the lower half of the refrigerator to the task of deep-freezing his evening and morning repasts. Tom searched for his favorite, pulled pork, baked beans, and fried apple meal. He always left one in an easy-to-get-to place so Monday would end with a whimper and not with a wail.

The microwave stood proudly at the far end of the center counter, facing the kitchen. Below and against the adjacent wall were the trash and recycle bins. Tom tried to help out on the recyclable end of things but had lost heart after hearing that China was no longer taking millions of tons of plastic and paper, this apparently due to our general disregard for rinsing animal and vegetable matter off the material before shipping the whole fetid mess off in some airless freight container across the globe. Up until now he had done what he could.

For all he knew the stuff was now being used as land fill, illegally redirected for use in the building up of the thousands of miles of levies that surrounded the continuously disappearing wetlands to the south. People in Louisiana generally didn't care how things got done, as long as they got done and that someone made bank on the deal. The good citizens of New Orleans, for sure, didn't want to know. Water management was priority here. Environmental disasters had always been the talk of the town, and recent flooding was the focus of yet another decade of improvements to the forever overwhelmed sewerage and water system.

Tom sighed, decided he was thinking too much, put the unwrapped plastic dish in the microwave and set the timer.

After a good stir and a second go around, the hot meal was carefully removed and centered on the coffee table in the living room.

Two two-liter bottles of Diet Coke and Dr. Pepper chilled in a lower door shelf of the fridge. He took out the Dr. Pepper and poured some over the glass of ice he had prepared while waiting on the final heating of the meal. A fork and paper napkin had also been laid out.

Now he sat contentedly, reached for the remote and snapped on the first of four shows he would watch before showering and then applying the icy-hot.

It was nearly one A.M. when the cat's insistence on going outside became loud enough to rouse Tom, who was stretched out on the couch with an ancient episode of Star Trek droning on in the otherwise darkened house.

Tom pushed himself up, powered down the remote, and made his way slowly to the back door. The cat bounced out for her nightly prowl. Tom pulled the screen then the hardwood door securely shut, locking it as he made for the bathroom.

After a quick shower, Tom went to his room, put on a clean t-shirt and boxer shorts and reached for the ointment kept on the bed-side table next to the lamp and alarm clock. He let out a small moan as he massaged the cream into his lower back.

At this point he was all but oblivious to the world until he heard the most frightful screech from a cat that he had ever heard. He jumped to his feet and raced to the back door, the direction from which the shrill cry had emanated. Twisting the bolt lock, he pushed through both doors, standing half dressed in the middle of his back yard, heart pounding. Rachel was nowhere to be seen.

He was certain it was his cat that was in distress. Where was she? He pressed further into the yard, now noting that the side door to the garage was slightly ajar. He must have left it open when he put the lawn mower back inside last Saturday. He crept up to the door, thinking a possum or raccoon may have slipped in, surprising the cat somehow.

Tom flipped the light switch just inside the door, blinded for an instant by the two rows of florescent lights that hung suspended from the center of the exposed wooden ceiling. When his eyes adjusted, he looked around but saw nothing out of place. Again, he listened, then switched the light back off, pulled the garage door shut and retraced his steps to the house. He continued calling the cat's name as he went. As he opened the screen door, Rachel tore past him and fled somewhere into the interior of the small domicile.

Tom jumped and swore, nearly tripping on the animal as he topped the last of the three entry steps.

"You almost gave me a heart attack, Rachel, what the heck?" he said, purposefully trying to calm himself down.

Tom pulled the door shut; making sure it was secure, then made his way through the darkened house and crawled into bed. He was thankful Rachel had come in, apparently unharmed, and, likewise, that the dull ache in his back was quickly fading away with the penetration of the muscle relaxing ointment. In minutes he was fast asleep.

Coffee and a microwavable sausage, cheese, and egg croissant got him off to work the next morning. Early on in the day he decided that he should take a closer look at the garage. Since the door had been unlocked it was possible that someone had slipped in meaning to make off with something of value. Tom knew that there wasn't much along those lines, but figured he'd check just the same.

It was Tuesday. Sally would get off of work at five, go home and soak in a bubble bath for two hours before coming over, as was her routine. She would show up around 7:30.

Tom would kill time waiting on her and his dinner by doing his laundry and rechecking the garage at the same time. As for the rest of his work day, it would tediously tic on and on as the dull ache in his hunched back slowly returned.

The twenty minute drive in a 2005 Honda Civic from the CBD to the river-bend was uneventful. The sky was grey, overcast and threatening to rain. This was a daily possibility on the gulf coast. He pulled into his drive just as the first burst of fat drops plopped onto his windshield. Tom sighed and pulled his ever-present umbrella from the floor on the passenger side of the car. Other than quick hot showers, Tom hated getting wet.

The umbrella popped open and Tom quickly made for the front porch. Shaking the water off and putting the umbrella in an ever-waiting umbrella stand under the mailbox, Tom checked the small rusty black receptacle. It was empty. Tom unlocked the front door. Rachel had magically appeared and crossed the threshold before he could close the heavy wooden door.

"What was up with you last night?" Tom intoned to a cat that was now sauntering just in front of him to the food dish in the kitchen. The cat meowed a feline reply.

Tom filled the dish, replaced the food in the cabinet and opened the back door. The rain added to the overall humidity but the temperature would be down a degree or two. Tom stood staring vacantly into the seldom used back yard. He had a bar-b-que grill in the garage but hadn't brought it out since his father had passed away. Even then it was his father's thing to do. Grilled burgers, hot dogs, chicken, and even the occasional slab of steak had graced the top of that grill. Tom shook his head, regretting the melancholy memory.

The thought of food made his mouth water, though, and he was startled when Rachel suddenly abandoned her eating and pressed up against his right shin. He ran his hand down the black cat's back and just as abruptly said, "Let's get the laundry started."

Tom went to his bedroom and pulled the linen off of the bed. In the summer it consisted of two sheets. He topped off the dirty clothes hamper with a pair of socks from the floor and three dress shirts and a pair of grey slacks that had casually been thrown on the mauve stuffed chair in the corner. Next, he plopped the hamper down in the hall and rounded up a couple of towels and a washcloth from the bathroom, tossing them in and continuing his rounds. Passing through the kitchen, he grabbed a utility towel from the door handle of the refrigerator and stuffed it under the wicker lid.

The drizzly sky made him wince as he started to make a dash for the garage. If the rain became more pronounced he would be trapped out there. He put down the hamper and made for the front porch. Umbrella in his right hand he now snatched up the thatched hamper, clutching it to his chest with his right arm and pushed past the screen door. Thumbing the umbrella button, Tom acrobatically popped the cloth shield open and raised it over his head.

Carefully he made his way down the three back steps and navigated the flagstone walk, now positioning himself under the small door awning for protection while he put down the basket and refolded the umbrella, carefully placing it just outside the door. Removing the keys from his pocket he let himself into the ever damp and oily smelling garage.

Just inside the door on the right was a small closet boxing in the water heater. Hot and cold water pipes ran over his head and were laid out to accommodate a washer, dryer, and a deep cast-iron wash basin on the left side of the door. The back wall and half of the opposite wall consisted of built-in floor-to-ceiling shelves. The shelves were jammed with a variety of odds and ends, with no apparent order or organization. There were the typical auto lubricants, old and unused small household appliances, an open plastic basket of Christmas decorations, a half dozen partially used gallon cans of paint and dozens of unmarked cardboard boxes of various shapes and sizes into which he had probably only looked once. There was one window above the sink and another over a flat work bench opposite the washer and dryer.

Tom put the hamper down in front of the washer and flipped on the overhead light switch. A short hum and the florescent lights flickered on. Getting back into the laundry routine, he pulled out the permanent press clothes and the two sheets and put them in the washer for the first load. He checked the settings, added the detergent and liquid softener that always sat on top of the beige front-loading companion dryer and hit the start button.

There would always be only two loads of laundry. He never did more. It would be twenty minutes for the first load. While those dried, he would run the second load through and in just over two hours the task would be complete. Sally would be over by then and he could settle down with her on the couch to make an evening of it. The convenience of the frozen dinners would make for a smooth transition while he would ask the compulsory, "How was your day?" and she would give him the long or short of it without bothering to inquire about his day in return.

Tom did not feel tired but there was a weariness about him that he could not shake off. Absent mindedly he stared out the open side entrance and watched the rain fall for nearly five minutes without moving. The washer was now sloshing softly in its first wash cycle when Tom heard an odd sound that was not coming from the machine next to him.

It was kind of a cross between the sound of a coffee maker hissing and the bubbling of a stew his mother might have made. There was no cooking smell however, and the sound seemed to be emanating from the wash basin.

Tom shook himself from his mental time-out and turned toward the deep sink. The sound continued, now slightly louder, as if trying to attract his attention. He slowly walked over, thinking it might be a backup of the drainage system. He certainly did not need a big plumbing bill. What he did need was a new car. He sighed.

Sure enough, the bottom quarter of the sink was filled with an inky black substance. It was undulating slightly but there was no sludge residue where it touched the sides of the sink. The liquid seemed to become more active, with bubbles and ripples crisscrossing the surface.

Tom swore to himself and found a nearby plunger, reserved for just such occasions. He seated the plumber's tool over the drain and proceeded to try to clear the apparent clog. As he pushed forcefully downward with both hands gripping the short wooden handle the liquid seemed to pull back and away from the plunger, leaving it and the center of the bottom of the sink perfectly clean.

What happened next was beyond belief. In the blink of an eye, the liquid transformed into a swarm of scurrying roaches, who in an effort to avoid the plunger's assault, poured out of the basin and hit the floor, spilling into a semicircle around Tom's feet.

He was stupefied and scared, all at the same time. Letting out a whimper, he backed toward the door, stomping his feet at the bugs that seemed to be able to counter his every footfall, all the while continuing to crowd in around him. Tom was hysterical and if anyone had been there to witness the event they would have thought he was either trying out the steps of some aboriginal war dance or trying to stomp out some non-existent fire.

Seconds had passed when suddenly the bugs retreated slightly, clumped together and reformed as six brown squirrels. Each eyed him tentatively, tails and whiskers twitching but fearless, none-the-less, watching the human continue to stumble backward toward the door.

The near-instantaneous transformation of the cockroaches to the squirrels got a, "What the fu...", from Tom, who was now blinking and rubbing his eyes thinking somehow someone at work had slipped him some kind of hallucinogenic drug. Brendon, known for his crude pranks, had been in the break-room just before Tom drew his final cup of coffee, around 3 p.m. He wondered how long it usually took for LSD or some similar intoxicant to kick in. This had to be some stupid practical joke.

Tom was now dead center in the doorway. The rain was steady at his back. He wanted to locate his umbrella but was afraid to take his eyes off of the innocent-looking little tree-dwellers. Tentatively, they began moving toward him. He felt like they were all watching him, waiting for him to react to their presence.

"Holy shit!" Another scream escaped Tom's lips as Rachel, who had followed him out the back door earlier, now decided to prance into the garage to see what all of the commotion was about.

"What the hell, cat!" Tom scolded the unsuspecting animal. He looked down again as the cat pressed up against his ankles, and then, upon seeing the cluster of squirrels, arched its back slightly and made ready to pounce.

Tom's eyes went from cat to squirrels and started babbling, "No, no, nooooo," upon seeing the next transformation. The bushy-tailed rodents seemed to jump into each other until only one black cat remained. It was Rachel, but Rachel, upon seeing the bizarre transformation herself had let out a fearful yowl and high-tailed it out of the garage.

Tom was so frazzled that he could only react by turning, grabbing up the umbrella, and running to the house. There was no time to open the umbrella and the rain drenched him thoroughly. He opened and shut both of the back doors with a couplet of malicious slams that reverberated down the block. Still unsure of his current state of mind he went into the bathroom and slammed that door shut, stripping off his wet dress shirt.

In a knee-jerk reaction he decided to throw himself onto the toilet and void any possible toxin in any way possible. He had seen his face in the mirror. It was beet red. His hair was dripping wet, but that was of no consequence at this point. He was certain that he was about to have a heart attack or a stroke and that some terrible end was upon him.

Tom sat on that toilet, unmoving for a very long time. Nothing changed form. He was not becoming nauseous. There was no searing headache or stomach pain, no need to initiate further medical action, nothing.

It was 7:37 when Sally knocked on the front door, her usual three sharp raps. Tom rose still shaking, pulled up his wet pants, flushed the toilet and reluctantly made his way to the front door.

As soon as he opened the door she noted his pale, flush features and for the first time in a long time actually asked, "Are you okay?"

He just stood there as Rachel came up behind her and quickly darted through the doorway. Tom remained speechless, as she moved past him and into the living room. Rachel ran straight to her food dish and resumed her evening meal.

Sally could see beads of sweat around Tom's hairline. She knew he seldom did anything to over-exert himself.

And then Sally reverted to her "me first" litany. "Are we going to have to take you to the emergency room? And after my horrible day, that's all I need tonight. I can't tell you how hard it was just to get to the end of my shift. Mr. Grey was, as usual, leering about and trying to get me alone with him in the back of the stock room. Claimed I had forgotten to put out a second box of Halloween candy. I had just put out the first and there was no room, for crying out loud. And he's all up in my face. I know he wants to grope me, and would if he could, the little parasite!"

Taking further control, she pulled Tom over to the couch and made him sit.

"Did you finish the laundry? I hope you put fresh sheets on the bed. Really Tom, I'm half out of my mind trying to have any kind of civilized conversation with my mother. She keeps insisting that she shouldn't have to work herself to death and how, now it's up to me to contribute more of this and that. What is the alternative, after all? Is she trying to drive me away, or what? Oh Tom…"

Tom, meanwhile, was beginning to regain some sense of normalcy. He was staring at her, without comment, as was his usual tact. Ok, so the tornado had returned to his house, he was no longer in Oz, but back in black and white Kansas.

He started to interject his mind-boggling vision but decided instead to fend off her Emergency Room inclinations. "I'm feeling better now," he said meekly. "I'm afraid the laundry didn't come off too well. I haven't been back out to the garage to put the first load into the dryer and start the second load. I kinda got," he thought carefully, "dizzy. I think I must have drunk one cup too many of that shop coffee. Sometimes I think I need to give it up and spare my heart the grief..."

"So, you've just been sitting around doing nothing, huh?" There was an accusatory tone now replacing the quasi-sympathetic dialogue. "Go on out and finish what you started. I'll fix us our dinner and you can relax watching, *Who Wants to Marry a Millionaire*? I think Joyce is going to be a very lucky girl tonight. Robert will propose, you wait, you'll see."

Tom moved in close enough to look out the curtained back door window and then nervously down at the eating cat. The rain had stopped briefly but he took up the umbrella he had hastily dropped inside the back door, just in case it started up again.

He paused briefly at the half-open garage entrance. Tentatively, he peeked inside. Nothing was amiss. The washer was silent, having finished the first load over an hour ago. He quickly made the exchange, filling the dryer and starting the second load. He was out the door, umbrella in hand in less than two minutes.

As he re-entered the back door, Rachel slipped past him, going out for her nightly prowl. He shook his head and Sally, remote in hand and TV on, said, "Come on, sit and eat, we've nearly missed last week's recap."

She had microwaved two spaghetti and meatball dinners. A tall glass of Dr. Pepper sat next to his meal. She scooped up her Diet Coke as he sat down, taking a second satisfying sip off the top of the jostling ice cubes that filled most of her 16 ounce plastic tumbler.

Tom sat, stared into space for over a minute, then bent to take the first bite of his dinner. Sally didn't notice. She was in the midst of her commentary narrative, something Tom always reacted to with the obligatory, "Yes" or "uh huh" or "really?" as if he were actually paying any attention to the show or her.

When both had finished their meals and drinks, Sally actually gathered up the plastic dishes and the eating utensils, ferrying them back to the kitchen. During the commercial break she refilled the soda glasses and sat down contentedly at Tom's side. She was now staring at him with a half smile and suddenly kissed him lightly on the cheek.

Tom knew this purposeful performance and waited to find out what would soon follow, usually a request for something she wanted.

"Tommy,, she began, not knowing that it was a nickname Tom loathed, "Can I stay over? Mom has been impossible…"

Tom could see her eyes refocusing on the TV screen as the show commenced. "Please. I'll never get a decent night's sleep in that house. I'll even help make the bed."

Tom wasn't at all sure if he wanted company but considered the possibility of a flashback and the need for someone to drive him to the hospital if things got really out of hand.

"Sure," he relented and she immediately returned to her commentary.

"I thought sure he would ask Joyce this week. Damn those producers. They just love to stretch things out as far as they can."

"Uh huh."

Three hours later Tom rose and let Sally know he was going to be in the bathroom for a shower. He had already finished the laundry, bringing the two loads in without further incident. She said nothing, having focused her attention on the 11 o'clock newscast.

Tom stood inside the bathroom for five minutes before deciding that the drenching he had gotten earlier was more than enough water for one day. After using the toilet he brushed his teeth and then went to his bedroom. Changing his underclothes he plodded back out to the living room.

Sally was sitting on the couch, Rachel on her lap.

"Didn't Rachel go out for the night?"

"Yes, but I heard her scratching to come back in, probably sensing a stormy night ahead. The weatherman says there's a fifty percent chance for thunderstorms until mid-morning." She looked up and Rachel hopped to the floor.

Tom stared at her. She sat like some Egyptian statue, eyes now fixed on him.

"She's not sleeping on the bed."

"Whatever, I'll be in in a minute," she said, prompting him to go on to bed. She had, true to her word, made it up during an earlier commercial break.

The cat remained where it sat and Tom pulled the bedroom door shut as he went inside. Still feeling some mild discomfort over the evening's events he went to the closet and pulled a thin blanket out, spreading it over the sheets.

Sally entered and in the dark removed her shoes, socks, blouse and skirt and slid into bed beside him. Not wishing to feel any sort of rejection, Tom decided not to approach her for sex. To his surprise she rolled over, putting her head on his chest and began stroking his face. He pulled her into his body, quickly excited by the warmth. As he rolled her onto her back and began to climb on top he paused to anxiously check the door. They both wiggled to remove their clothing under the covers and in the dark.

"The day could have ended much worse," he thought to himself as she began moaning softly.

The next morning Tom woke first and went into the kitchen to start coffee brewing. As he passed the corner of the living room he was suddenly puzzled to see that Rachel was still sitting in the exact same place she had been the night before. Her eyes blinked and her whiskers twitched slightly as she watched him pass.

She then walked to the back door and looked up expectantly, waiting to be let out. Tom obliged. He couldn't help thinking, though, that this was not the cat's usual routine. As he opened the inner door and then pushed the screen door open, Rachel went out, disappearing around the corner of the house. But before he could close the door Rachel raced back in, coming from the same direction, fur wet and matted. She went straight to her food dish and began eating the few remaining morsels at the bottom.

Tom shook his head, pulling the doors shut and turning to stare at the perplexing animal. Sally came plodding in at that moment, dressed but shoeless, hair askew. Tom had not heard her come up behind him and literally jumped when she touched his shoulder.

"Sally! Oh my god Sally, I didn't mean to shout but you startled me."

"You big fraidy cat," she teased. "Is the coffee on?"

"It'll be a minute."

Sally went into the living room, scooped up the remote and switched on a morning show. The hosts were talking about a new pair of panda cubs, born at the San Diego zoo last night.

An hour later they were both off to their places of work. Tom glared at Brendon all day. Brendon actually shrugged his shoulders at one point and said, "What did I do?" Tom took this as a veiled admission of guilt but made no reply, feeling for a moment as if the bizarre events of the previous day could have been the result of indigestion or an overworked mind.

The evening was overcast but dry as he put the key into his front door lock. As he turned the key Rachel showed up like clockwork, ready for the night-time routine. He reached down tentatively to pat her head and she purred loudly in response.

Wednesday was his day to study. After feeding the cat, Tom went in and switched on the desktop computer then returned to the kitchen to get out a chicken pot pie for the evening's meal. He removed the packaging, punched holes in the pie's crust, and shoved it into the microwave.

Five minutes later he heard a faint scuffing at the back door. Tom had been in the study logging onto the CPA instructional website. He returned to the kitchen, only to see Rachel now lapping water from her water bowl. The scratching noise, emanating from somewhere outside of the back door, grew louder and more persistent.

Tom peered cautiously out of the curtained window and then decided to scan the backyard from the safety of a closed screen door. As he pulled the inner door open the sound grew even more frantic. Curiosity, and being in the relative safety of

126

his own house, Tom pushed the outer door open, barely six inches when in ran Rachel, zipping over his feet and darting into the living room.

Rachel, still at her food bowl noted the sudden intrusion and darted out of the house, squeezing past the outer door that was now nearly shut. Tom had spun around, eyes on the newcomer. The obsidian furred feline went to the same spot it had frozen itself into on the previous evening. It now sat, sphinx-like. Tom stared at the animal for a full two minutes, not certain what to do next.

Tom's brain had now gone into overdrive. He could only guess as to what was happening but he wanted to know exactly what that "what" was. It was at this point that his inquisitiveness overcame his seemingly irrational fear. He resolved to do something that some would-be onlooker might consider crazy. But Tom was now certain that he wasn't crazy.

He stammered at the unmoving creature, "What, what the hell are you?"

The cat's head turned slowly, now facing up at the towering human. "I am Soli."

A shiver rippled down Tom's spine and once again he nearly jumped out of his skin as the timer bell on the microwave indicated that the pot pie was cooked.

"Please do not be afraid," the voice was coming from the duplicate Rachel. It seemed to resonate as a human voice in his ear, eerily familiar. Then there was a soft moan. It was Sally's moan and it made Tom take a step backward.

"Tommy," the cat now stood on its hind legs and began to walk toward him.

"Oh my god! Oh my god!" Tom wailed and the cat immediately dropped down on its four legs. Rachel Number Two sat, recreated the statuesque pose and waited patiently for him to regain his composure.

"What are you?" he repeated, this time not quite sure he wanted to know the answer.

"I am Soli," the cat repeated and then began to grow and transform, becoming the perfect double of Sally, clad only in her bra and underwear.

Tom was both frightened and amazed. He was not losing his mind. He had been at work. He had successfully driven home. He was in the middle of his Wednesday night routine, for crying out loud.

"Sally?"

"Soli," the entity whispered as if not wanting to spook a wild deer. "I will not hurt you. Please, do not be afraid."

"Are you a ghost? Am I going mad?" Unnerved he could think of nothing else to do but run into his study and log onto the Internet, furiously typing in the search window, "apparitions, ghosts, cats, bugs, phantoms, aliens..."

He pressed "enter" only to get a listing of web pages related to finding these items on ebay, psychic phenomena, U.F.O. sightings, and addresses to companies selling Halloween costumes. He looked up at her. She stood in the hall, mouth closed but eyes wide open and fixed on him.

"I am a traveler," the Sally look-alike intoned. Tom noticed with increasing irritation that she was not speaking with her mouth. Her lips never parted. There was the slightest hint of a smile on them, however.

"Is this some kind of a sick joke?" he finally lambasted the specter.

"Sick joke? What is a sick joke? I am just learning, just beginning to understand your language, your communication system."

"You're an alien! I knew it! You are some kind of creature from outer-space!" Tom was not sure that this idea made him feel any more reassured about the situation at hand.

"Whatever you are, you've you taken over Sally's body. Is she still in there? Are you a body snatcher?" He started to Google body snatcher but thought better of it. In that same instance Soli morphed again, this time returning to the form of Rachel.

"This form doesn't seem to upset you as much. Should I stay in this form?"

It was at this point that Tom began to feel himself actually beginning to relax. He wasn't sure why he should be inclined to do so. All his inner instincts were screaming for him to dial 911. He pushed those inclinations aside but pulled his cell phone out of his back pocket and laid it on the desk, just in case.

This thing, what ever it was, was trying to communicate with him. It was doing whatever it thought necessary to allay his fears. And in all reality, if that could be applied, it had not turned into a giant monster intent on killing, abducting, or probing him, at least not yet. It was not some menacing blob of black that aimed to consume him, although it had certainly started out as one. He considered that the roaches and squirrels could have been seen as familiar creatures and had not been meant to appear menacing as his own reaction to them would otherwise indicate. This Soli thing was going out of its way to represent itself as non-threatening.

The black cat now turned around and walked back into the kitchen. "Come, get your nourishment. Your food is waiting."

Tom, still dumb-founded, immediately realized that he was, indeed, hungry and eyed the microwave which had been beeping its reminder signal in the background all the while.

"How are you talking to me?" he ventured as he took two oven mitts and removed the hot pie from the small electric oven.

"The same way that you have cooked your meal," Rachel responded. "Everything is done through waves, microwaves, sound waves, light waves, this is the essence of the universe. This is also the essence of what I am. By changing the frequency of my vibrations I can form myself into what ever I can perceive. My ability to see things is, of course, not the same as yours. I must encompass something before I can perceive it. You might say I need to wrap myself around things in order to see them."

Hesitantly, Tom took the pie to the kitchen counter, retrieved a fork from a drawer next to the sink, grabbed a paper towel and a Mardi Gras cup, placing them both on the counter next to the pot pie. He then grabbed the Dr. Pepper out of the refrigerator and brought it with him to the high table, pulling up a barstool and planting himself squarely upon it.

Rachel Number Two jumped up on the second stool and resumed the sitting cat pose.

Tom, now feeling as though he had not eaten for days, poured himself a glass of soda and began to dig into his pot pie. He tentatively looked over at the cat.

"I have travelled through the vast reaches of what you call space. I am an explorer, as you would say…"

"How are you learning our language? You said you were learning our language."

"I have been here for three of your weeks. I have acquired your language by translating the vibrations of the words that you and others have spoken and by monitoring your audio and video transmission devices. After having established the origins of your words, I have delved into your brain, and those of others to read your neuropathic thoughts.

"All things are variations of wave frequencies. The amplitude of modulation and the actual number of these waves overlapping, coming together or dispersing is the basis for your perception of gasses, liquids, solids, and plasma. I simply have the ability to discern your vibrations, separating your so-called physical nature from your cognoscente intent. Every sentient being that I have encountered on my journey has a means of communicating, some much more sophisticated than others."

Tom eagerly woofed down the small dinner and guzzled down his Dr. Pepper. This was fantastic. He had finally come to the realization that he was actually talking to an alien being, something that had arrived from another world. For all he knew, he may be the only living human in history to have this distinct honor. Of course it was an honor. It had to be an honor. Somehow fate had granted him an experience that no other could look down upon. He would be a celebrity. He would be world renowned as the first man on earth to greet a newcomer from another planet.

"I am not exactly from a planet," the cat interjected. Tom swiveled his chair to look over at the alien.

"Cool," he said, "you're reading my mind!"

"You could say I am a planet, or a star, or the very substance of space itself."

"Well, that's a bit confusing," Tom responded, feeling a slight sense that this experience was by far more overwhelming than what he was allowing it to be. "How can I tell others about you if I can't pin down what you are or where you've come from? Is this some kind of inter-dimensional experience?"

"No one must know that I am here, Tommy."

"Please don't call me that. Only Sally calls me that and in all honesty, I hate it."

"Sorry," Soli said softly, intent on conveying his or her true remorse. "I thought you responded in a positive way to this name spoken by Sally."

"Tom, just call me Tom."

"Tom, no one must know I am here. I should not even be communicating with you but I have been travelling for such a long time. I needed to engage with something more vibrant than a rock, if you know what I mean. Your neighbors did not feel as intellectually or emotionally satisfying as you do, despite your initial fears. I felt you to be a gentle entity with little of the agitation many of the so-called living creatures on this planet tend to exhibit.

"For some reason other life-forms do not understand or have the intellectual capacity to inhibit their natural instincts toward a fight or flight reaction to my presence," the cat apparition added.

"Ok, two things: are you male or female and are you one or are there others here with you?" Tom's curiosity continued to fuel the dialogue between him and the unknown. He felt like a kid at Christmas. He was interacting with a species never before seen or even dreamed of by his fellow human beings!

"I can be whatever you wish to perceive me as. I am, as is everything seen and unseen, a composite of waves. I can be the expression of one wave or the accumulation of many. In essence I can be whatever I choose to be at any given moment in time."

With that, the black cat suddenly jumped from its perch, transforming into the Dell table-top computer, which now sat squarely in the middle of the kitchen floor.

Inspired by this event, Tom wiped his mouth with the paper napkin, rose from his seat, and returned to the study. The desktop on the kitchen floor reverted to the cat and followed. He sat at the small desk now and typed "Michael Jordan" into the search engine at the top of the screen. From the results page he selected "images." He clicked on a shot of Michael dunking a basketball during the final minutes of a championship game.

The cat jumped up on the desk and watched Tom's curious actions, taking it all in stride.

"Make yourself into this guy," Tom quipped, as if he had just invented a new interstellar game. His finger tapped the screen.

Rachel Number Two responded by jumping off the desk and forming into a likeness of the player, feet in the air and arm arched with the trajectory of an absent basketball.

Tom actually laughed out loud, standing up to take in the full stature of the basketball superstar. The figure hovered, eight inches above the floor, unmoving. Tom walked around to the side of the figure only to see that there was no side. The reproduction was completely two dimensional, as it was on the computer screen.

He stuck his foot under the static player. It was in fact, floating in mid-air. He poked a finger at the visible side and found it to be solid, as hard as the glass computer screen from which it had been resurrected.

With a liquid-like exchange the player reverted to the small black animal, now sitting patiently at Tom's feet. They stared at each other intently for a long minute. Something occurred to Tom which kind of unnerved him again.

"Does this mean that you wrapped yourself around Sally last night?"

The cat bubbled up into Sally's likeness once again, lips closed but smiling a bit more than before.

"And me? Did you see me the same way?"

Sally morphed into Tom. The two stood toe to toe. Then, just as suddenly, the alien minx returned to Sally's likeness. "Yes," she said, without moving her lips.

"And you were in the room when Sally and I made love?"

"There did not seem to be too much love involved in your sexual intercourse," replica Sally said, a little too smugly.

"That's beside the point," Tom continued, his cheeks reddening. "I shut the door. You were sitting in the living room."

"Until you shut the door, yes. Then I became vaporous and slipped in under the portal. I remained in that invisible state until you both fell asleep. At that point I left the room and actually went back outside to roam the neighborhood, learning more about the nature of your humanness. I have also been 'studying,' for want of a better word, the other plants and animals that inhabit your perceived world. You are a curious lot, all the things that you allow to exist in your consciousness. It never ceases to amaze me how such free-flowing entities can tie themselves down to an existence filled with things that frighten, induce anger, or imprison the spirit. You are like children believing in monsters."

Suddenly the introspective mood was broken by three loud raps on the front door.

Tom shot a look at the Sally duplicate, who was still clad in only her white cotton underwear. "Oh my god, it's Sally!" He crossed the hall and anxiously looked to the front door. The three knocks were repeated, a bit louder this time.

"She can't be a part of this. She would never understand. I need to get rid of her somehow." With this, he waved Sally Number Two back into the study and pulled the door shut.

133

"Coming," he called out. Seconds later he opened the front door but not wide enough to allow Sally to come inside. She had an impatient look on her face. "You know this is my study day Sally. What do you want?"

Sally took a step back, her face reddening. "Tommy…"

"Please Sally," Tom didn't want to come off as too confronting. "Can't you call later?" He found himself stepping out of the house and onto the front porch.

"Mom and I are…"

Tom found himself suddenly uncharacteristically assertive. "Sally, you and your mom are always fighting. What's new? I need to study. I am already a chapter behind. I want to take my C.P.A. exam in December, remember? We had an understanding about your visits, didn't we? Tonight is not a good night." Tom stepped back across the threshold, drawing the door inward. "Call me later, we'll talk."

Without hesitating he pulled the door shut.

Sally was struck dumb. This was not the Tom she knew. This was someone being mean to her for no good reason. She looked around herself in bewilderment. Had something changed? Then it occurred to her that he might be hiding something. She latched onto that idea and took it one step further. What, exactly was he hiding?

Sally reached forward, intent on knocking on the door again but thought better of it. There was something going on in there and the best way to find out was to get a quick look through his study window. She hoped the curtains would be open enough for her to catch a glimpse of him doing whatever it was that he was doing.

Not caring whether the neighbors would catch her peeping into her boyfriend's window she turned and walked around to the side of the house. With a furtive glance around she approached the side of the window and then cautiously moved toward the three inch slit between the thin blue curtains.

She let out a gasp as she looked in upon Tom who was talking to another woman. No, not just another woman, it was her, clad only in panties and braw, sitting in the chair behind his

134

desk. Sally ducked away but could not help returning her gaze to the astonishing scene. The lady in the chair sat perfectly still. There was no movement on her part, although Tom, barely audible, continued to talk to her.

It was a doll, she concluded. Somehow he had gotten a hold of a sex doll to replace her! Sadness and anger raged up inside her. She wanted to confront him. She needed to confront him. She marched around to the front door.

Sally Number Two had felt her presence at the window and now warned Tom. "She's coming back and she is angry."

"What?" Tom stammered. Then, "Hide!"

A loud banging now erupted at the front door. Sally Number Two reconstituted herself as Rachel Number Two and padded into the kitchen where she then sat motionless next to her food bowl.

Tom opened the front door trying to appear upset by the new intrusion. He swung the door open only to be slapped by the charging Sally who pushed him aside, making for the study.

Rachel, who had heard the commotion, took advantage of the open door and sauntered back inside behind her. There was definitely some clamoring going on so she moved quickly into the living room, positioning herself at the far end of the couch.

"Where is it?" Sally insisted, immediately determining that the life-sized doll had been moved. "You pervert, you heartless son of a bitch!"

"Sally." Tom stepped in front of her and tried to turn her around, wanting in vain to get her back out the front door.

"I saw her... it!" Sally screeched. You would rather keep company with a blowup doll than spend time with me. This is unbelievable. And after all I've given you." Uncertain as to the depth of her feelings, Tom stopped for a moment, witnessing what appeared to be tears in his girl friend's eyes. She had cried before at the end of a sad movie, now and then, but that had been the extent of that emotional outpouring. Tom was caught completely off guard. He did not want to think of himself as being cruel.

Sally took advantage of his hesitation and swung around, pulling open the sliding door of the walk-in closet. Seeing nothing she tore past him and into the master bedroom and finally into the bathroom, peering cautiously behind the shower curtain.

Angry and confused Sally now saw herself as being some crazed lady, having imagined the whole thing. She came back into the living room and plopped down on the couch. Rachel moved cautiously toward her purring loudly and eager for a cessation in the unexpected chaos.

"I, I just wanted to know if I could spend another night here," she began sobbing.

Tom, standing in the archway of the hall, now stared at her without expression. She had wanted something from him. He had not given in to her demands. She had then become hysterical. This was not something that the thirty-four-year-old bookkeeper wanted to deal with now or in the future.

"Please leave," he said firmly.

She rose, somewhat shakily and started to move toward him.

"Please leave," he repeated, approaching her with an outstretched, guiding hand.

As Sally stood up and took two steps toward him, she saw Rachel Number Two sitting motionless near the empty cat-food bowl and let out a surprised squeal on seeing the second Rachel. Hoping to change the subject she quipped, "Look Tom there's another cat that looks just like your Rachel. It must have come in when we left the door open."

Tom did not hesitate. "Call me later. We can talk about all of this later." He then scooped up Rachel and putting his other arm around Sally's waist firmly guided her back out of the front door. He then said to Sally, "Be nice to your mom," turned around and went back inside, pulling the door shut behind him.

Tom stood behind the closed door, heart pounding. He heard the engine of Sally's Toyota rev up and then it moved away. Rachel wiggled free from his grasp, hopped down to the floor and wandered back into the kitchen. Upon seeing her cloned double she arched her back and hissed suspiciously. Rachel Number Two vaporized, disappearing in a thin wisp of mist.

"Why do I put up with her?" Tom turned to address the cat that wasn't there. Rachel now stood at the back door, obviously wanting to go back outside. Tom reached down and grabbed her up. The cat let out a couple of meows and rubbed its head into his chest for reassurance. He petted the animal lovingly.

"Sorry Rachel," he said, taking note of the fact that the noise had come from an open mouth and that the throaty purring had resumed. "I need to tell Soli that she needs to find another form to duplicate so she doesn't freak you out so much. Where did she go, anyway?"

Tom opened the back doors and let the cat out. At the bottom of the steps Rachel stopped and looked back at him. Of all of the creatures in the world, Rachel was as close to a soul-mate as he'd ever gotten. "Everyone else," he thought to himself, "either wants to use me or wants nothing to do with me."

A second microwave suddenly appeared on the center counter.

"I cannot understand why life on this planet is so stubbornly rigid," Soli mused.

"Rigid?" Tom countered.

"Yes, you want to perceive yourself as something tangible, something that others like you should come to recognize, to acknowledge, and to love. Perhaps it has to do with the vast sea of space and time, and the desire to be solid and in one place even if for only for a handful of your earth decades. You want birthday parties, to increase in size over time and to grow old enough to have hair on your body. Most of you want to make small versions of yourself that will follow in the same footsteps. You want others to like the way you look, recognize the skills you acquire and to respect your wisdom as you get older. I do believe it has something to do with the electro-magnetic properties of this planet, this region of space, somehow."

Soli's words were slowly sinking into his otherwise overwhelmed brain. Life was a finite thing, after all. His was just getting started and most of the things Soli had listed as being lifetime milestones had yet to be realized in his own life.

Suddenly, Tom felt very lonely. He had just run off his only lady friend and he was now talking to an imaginary microwave. Shaking his head he walked back into the study and settled into the comfortable chair behind the desk.

Absently, he gazed out between the parted curtains. Tom closed his eyes and shook his head, realizing that this whole episode might end as quickly as it had begun. He began to question his own sanity again. What was happening here and why now? This alien thing had asserted itself into his life, into his brain. What hit him hardest, though, was his need to better know this mysterious visitor. There was something, something inside of him that he felt had begun to change in its presence.

He had no claim to Soli, no way to detain her. It also dawned on him that he had mentally labeled this alien being as a female, a female to whom he was finding himself strangely attracted. He stared at the computer screen on the desk in front of him. He scrolled the C.P.A. instructional text down to chapter 8 and began to read. As he began jotting notes on a legal pad Soli rematerialized into a small goldfish bowl, complete with goldfish. The fish now swam in lazy circles at the corner of his desk.

"A lady down the street has one. When she looks at it, it seems to calm her," Soli intoned softly.

Tom laughed and continued his studies for the next three hours. It took his mind off of other things, giving him the security of numbers, the only constants in an ever-changing world.

Now Tom was tired. He stared at the goldfish and realized that its mouth remained shut, unlike a real one that would constantly be gulping in water and air. He switched off the computer, grabbed up the small clear globe, turned out the light and headed for his bedroom. Gently he placed the fishbowl on the nightstand and switched on the small lamp beside it.

As he was toweling himself off following a quick shower, he paused to consider his "rigid" life. He was rooted pretty deep into his daily routines, of that there was little doubt. For a moment he wondered what life would be like without them.

Tom returned to the bedroom, put on clean undergarments and slid into bed. He thought about Sally now, and sighed. She would be beside him now, warm and inviting, or not. The fishbowl disintegrated and Soli reformed next to him under the sheet and light blanket.

"You can't be serious," Tom said, uncertain as to what he should do next.

"Feel your vibrations, Tom. Allow yourself to flow with them, to embrace any reality you choose. Pleasure always comes from within, it can be felt whenever you choose to feel it."

Tom felt himself compelled to touch this magical apparition. She was warm, soft, her body responsive to his advances. Unexpectedly, Tom felt her pull away from him. She sat up, unfastened the bra and it disappeared as it came away from her skin. As she slid back under the sheet she peeled away the cotton panties and they too evaporated.

Having sex two nights in a row with Sally was a rarity, to say the least. She would have, in fact, pulled her granny gown out of the closet for a second night's stay. It was her "hands off" signal and he had reluctantly learned to comply. Normally he would have settled for a few minutes of spooning and then rolled over to sleep.

Tonight rigid was going to work in his favor, he thought. He dived under the blanket and began kissing the softness of her belly. His hands stretched up to take each of her small breasts, kneading them gently. She let out a Sally moan and he was inspired. Even in the dark this was familiar territory so he continued to slide down to a soft, light brown tuft of hair. He breathed in the scent of her womanhood. He wondered how Soli

139

knew to include this pheromone-inspired detail. She squirmed beneath his advances.

Tom kissed her inner thighs but stopped short of going down on her, deciding instead to enhance the love part of lovemaking. He pulled himself up and on top of her, seeking the wet warmth of her lips. Passionately he pressed his to hers. Her lips did not part. He kissed Soli more deeply. Her naked breasts seemed to swell beneath his chest. He could hold himself away from her no longer.

Tom positioned himself for penetration. Although she was definitely wet on the outside, he could not seem to slip inside of her. Seconds later, he exhaled in frustration and allowed his weight to collapse gently upon her replicate body. There was no way inside this being from another planet. Looking sideways at the side of her head he now noticed that even her ears were not true orifices. Just inside the ear canal a blockage of skin sealed the channel. He now examined her more closely, the same held true for her nostrils and mouth.

Tom suddenly lost his nerve and gently rolled off of the warm skin. She looked over at him, a subdued sense of curiosity in her searching eyes.

"You are definitely not human," Tom lamented, trying to keep his disappointment at bay.

"I am not," she replied. "Do not be angry with me."

Tom's face was growing red. "What are you?" The strained tenor in his voice made Soli roll away from him, the movement preceding her transformation into a bright ball of plasma, now floating four feet above the bed.

"I cannot assimilate a true human form," she admitted. And then, almost apologetically she added, "I have felt the vibration of your planet. There are forces here that attract waves. The energies of your solar system were born from your thoughts, your wave patterns. Your reality has formed over millennia, forcing a reshaping of the local wave frequencies. Always there have been universal laws overseeing the formation of liquids, solids, gasses, and my natural preference, plasma. It would take me thousands of your earth years to reconstitute the music of your bodies, your plants, your animals. As I am, I can only provide you with a solid form, like a brick or block of wood. In essence, to you, in your world, I am like a marble statue with a thin surface of skin."

Tom slowly calmed himself and reluctantly pulled the covers over his lower torso. He felt such a fool for believing this thing could be anything remotely human. Now he wondered why she had led him to think she, or it, was something other than a visitor from another world.

"We are all connected, Tom. We need each other as much as you believe you need air in order to exist. I find myself wanting to change you, to take you out of your skin and bring you into my reality. The vibrations are almost overwhelming. I have never felt a pattern of waves so alluring, so promising..." the voice trailed off.

"Have you seen the neighbor's cat? Tom quipped, almost in jest. "You can be the neighbor's cat. Rachel seldom puts up a fuss when it hangs around the house. Just stay away from her food dish and we should be fine for the moment."

The glowing blue orb floated slowly down to the bed. A young calico cat now sat at the foot of the blanket. Tom sighed, pulled the covers up over his chest and rolled over to sleep. Soli cautiously moved closer, lying now at the center of his back.

"Can I stay a while longer?" Soli whispered. "Can I see the world through your eyes?"

"Sure," Tom replied and, yawning, closed his eyes to sleep.

The next morning, as Tom readied for work, he let Rachel back into the house. The two cats bumped noses for a brief greeting before Rachel made her way to the ever-waiting food and water dishes. Tom walked softly up behind the black cat, stooped and stroked the short hair on her back. The feline arched up, thankful for the attention.

"Mornin' Puss Puss," he said affectionately.

Meanwhile, Sofi had again transformed into Sally Number Two and was channel-surfing the television. She didn't seem to care what was happening on any given show, only that there were so many shows and it was impossible to watch them all at once.

Tom was finishing his coffee at the breakfast bar.

"The first thing we need to do is to get you into a new body. It has to be someone Sally doesn't know. Tell me again, how this whole duplication thing works."

"I must *feel* what I am to become, as you say. The outside surface is all that I need to envelope."

"Ok, you can be anything but Rachel or Sally until I get home from work. He pointed to the kitchen clock. When this instrument reads five zero zero, maybe a little after, I will be returning. Then I'll get food and we'll take a trip to a mall."

"Mall, an indoor shopping arena," she quoted, as if from a dictionary. "Yes, well, maybe we can find a new you at the mall."

Tom rinsed his cup in the sink and set it into the adjoining dish-rack. He smiled at the idea, turning to see Sally Number Two, apparently engrossed in a morning show cooking segment. He sighed.

It was time to leave. He had seen the day's weather earlier on TV, and now reminded himself not to forget his umbrella.

As he drove to work on yet another overcast morning, he thumbed on his smart-phone. There were twelve messages, all from Sally. He would read them on his first break. A heavy feeling passed over him. "What on earth am I doing?" he thought to himself.

Tom's work day was typical. In fact, as he sat at his desk tallying numbers and making notes on his spreadsheets, he realized that until Soli's arrival, he had not noticed how bland and uninspiring his work, no, his entire life, had become. It really had no substance, no width or depth to it. There was nothing really to look forward to, nothing really to get exited about. It was, in a word, dull. That is until Soli had awakened something deep inside of him, something he had never truly considered a part of this mundane existence.

Tom had known yearnings well enough. He was a real boy and had experienced lust. But he never considered himself significant or worthy enough to love or to be loved. He had never thought of himself as being vital or important in the eyes of the world. He was born a cog in the machine. He realized now that he had resigned himself to that fate. And even with a C.P.A. certification, his pathetic life would have shuffled along monotonously until the day he died.

Soli was a revelation, a spark from some distant and unknown universe. Even immersed in the anxiety of the Sally incident the previous day, this entity had made him feel more certain of himself, more worthy of a place in history, and not just the life of a placeholder.

Sally's texts conveyed nothing less than the full spectrum of human emotion. Anger, sadness, regret, even a hint of vulnerability, and then a swelling of indignation and a resumption of the accusations she had made at the house. The final letter scolded him for being such an insensitive louse. She finished the note saying that she did not know what she had seen in him over the past three years.

Tom deleted the messages and returned to his desk.

At 5:23 Tom shook the rain out of his umbrella and placed it in the rack beneath his mailbox. There was a fine mist in the air. He pulled a flier for auto insurance from the small black receptacle, closed its lid, then unlocked the door. Rachel purred at his feet.

Inside, a small goldfish bowl sat in the middle of the center counter. The hovering fish turned to look at Tom as he entered the house.

As was his routine, Tom first addressed the needs of his feline companion, filling both food and water dishes. They had a "meow, meow" chat. The cat audibly engaged Tom, as if in conversation. The exchange grounded Tom and he smiled appreciatively as his black companion settled into eating.

Tom now addressed the fish bowl.

"You told me you could become a liquid, a solid, a gas, or a ball of plasma, but how do you manage three of those things at once?" he queried. He then made a b-line for the freezer and pulled out a frozen dinner; fettuccini, broccoli, and chicken in a cream sauce.

"You do know that, you, yourself are made up of a combination of gasses, liquids, and solids," Soli's Sally voice floated on the air. "You may think that you are composed of billions of what you call molecules, but they are not as solid as you have chosen to picture them in your consciousness, your mind, as you call it. I am the same as you are but with no pre-conceived notions about what I must be.

"In truth, we are both waves of pure energy. The difference is that your waves have taken on a form. People, places, things; it is all about your perception. Your waves have gotten used to the idea of your world being the way that it is. I have no such illusions."

Tom popped the dish into the microwave and continued the dinner routine, getting out utensils and pouring his drink as he waited and listened patiently.

"Because you are fixed in the manner of your vibrations, your wave forms have conformed to your expectations. As I have mentioned, this part of your galaxy is prone to such things. The waves here resonate in more compact configurations, influenced by what you call your genetic building-blocks. These form what you perceive to be your bodies. The synergy of your collective beliefs define all of the things that live and grow around you. Actually, even the innate objects of the earth and your visible place in the universe are a manifestation of these same wave patterns. To keep it simple, I would say, you have come to like, or at least to tolerate what you understand to be your reality. It is, what you might call, your comfort zone."

"Could've fooled me," Tom said dryly. "I never found much comfort in it."

"That has been one of my biggest questions. Why do you insist on it being so?"

Tom shook his head, not understanding the question at all.

"Couldn't say. Not in charge of that shit!" he laughed wryly. "Anyway, let's talk about our trip to the mall." The microwave bell rang and he scooted the oblong plastic dish onto the counter with an insulated oven mitt.

"I must admit, I was taken with your 'Sally in her underwear' get up," Tom sheepishly acknowledged. "But like I told Rachel, we are going to have to find you another form if you are going to stay around for any length of time. Sally will be back sooner or later and we can't have the two of you staring each other down. Big trouble, big, big trouble," he said shaking his head. Tom now sat on a bar stool and took a sip of his cold drink, waiting for the meal to cool.

"We need to find someone from out of town. Maybe check license plates as cars roll into the parking garage. We need to play it cool. You know, not make a big fuss if we spot someone worth following. Stalkers get arrested at malls, ya know."

Soli had no idea what Tom was talking about but understood that he was forming a plan for their outing. The fishbowl vaporized and then reformed as a life-sized 2-D likeness of Vanna White, posed with outstretched hands, as if indicating revealed letters to game contestants.

Tom laughed out loud. "How did you learn to be so funny?"

"Joy is a higher form of vibration. It is a natural state of our existence."

"Ok, Einstein, enough with the theories of relativity." He began eating his meal with the gusto of an engineer shoveling coal into the belly of an old steam engine. In a manner of minutes the task was complete and he considered himself refueled. He finished the drink in the same manner; rose, rinsed the dishes and then disposed of the recyclable plastic food container.

"Well, you can't go like that," Tom chuckled again at the Wheel of Fortune image. "You will have to travel as Sally for now but you need to wear a pair of my sunglasses and my old grey fedora. Oh, and wear her dress and shoes, please. You can't go running around town barefoot and in your underwear."

Tom could have sworn he heard a giggle as Soli transformed, now standing next to him in his bedroom. Tom found sunglasses on the top of a small three shelf storage unit and then opened the walk-in closet on his side of the center dividing wall. Poking around for a few minutes he came out with a two hats and a trench-coat. He placed the fedora on her head. It slid down over her ears but did not cover her eyes. Tom put the shades on the bridge of her nose, adjusted them slightly, nodding his head in approval after looking her over, head to foot.

"Can you see alright?"

"I see everything," she quipped as he wrapped her in the trench-coat.

She was, Tom thought, incognito. "Great, let's go." He pulled on his green waterproof jacket and a Saints fleur-de-lis ball-cap that he had found for himself.

Cautiously he led the way out the front door. On the porch he scanned the quiet neighborhood. No one was walking the sidewalks as the rain continued its steady drizzle. He grabbed his umbrella and led Soli to the passenger side of the car. Unlocking the door he let her get inside before taking away the protective cover.

"The stores are open until nine this evening," Tom said as he climbed in, giving the umbrella a quick shake before pushing it into the back seat and pulling his door shut. Unsure of her reaction to the car ride he said, "We will be moving. Let me help you with your seat belt." A huge smile beamed out from under the undercover disguise. "What are you smiling at?" Tom could not resist and kissed her cheek. He then turned to start the car.

As he backed out of the short driveway she quipped, "We are always moving, Tom. Most humans tend to ignore that." She aimed another radiant smile his way.

As they drove across town, Tom explained that they needed to go somewhere the real Sally was not likely to be tonight. He was fairly certain that the weekend constituted her usual mall shopping habits, but wanted to take no chances. They would make their way to a mall in Slidell, half an hour away.

Like a tour guide, he pointed out landmarks along the way. Sally Number Two sat quietly, staring out the front window as the windshield wipers swished back and forth. Nearly thirty minutes later they entered the mall grounds, making their way to the second floor of a five story parking garage.

Before he got out of the car Tom gave his final instructions. "I know that you can whisper. Please keep your voice low and near my ears so others don't overhear our exchange of words. They may not understand what we are doing and I don't want them to figure it out. We are first going to walk around in the garage until we find someone to duplicate. We need to follow them for a while so we may need to go into the mall. Please stay close to me Soli. There will be lots of things to distract you." He had no real idea how Soli would react to the various window displays, the shoppers, or any other possible mall event, but like the male chauvinist he was raised to be, he thought it might be a girl thing. "Anyway, stay close and you can study our target, the person we select. If we think she is a good candidate, then you can duplicate her form and we will go home."

"I understand, Tom. Will this person be attracted to you? Will your vibrations caress?"

"What? No! I mean, maybe it could happen but not usually when two people first meet."

"I felt our connection the moment I sensed your presence. It is a natural thing."

Tom blushed. He wished it was a natural thing.

"We cannot say 'hello' or strike up a conversation. It might arouse suspicion and I don't want any trouble. This person must never know that you exist, remember? I think if she knew she might get upset, freak out or something. We can't take the chance."

147

With that, Tom exited the car, walking around to open the door for Soli. He leaned in to release her seatbelt and felt compelled to kiss her once again. Oh how he wished the real Sally could have been a mirror image of this extraterrestrial. Things would have been so much different if her "vibrations" had resonated more like Soli's.

As he closed the door and locked the car he stood silently beside this exotic reflection of an otherwise tedious personality. It occurred to him that he was now on a shopping quest. His mission was to find someone that suited him visually and in mannerisms.

He considered how much different his life would have been if he could have shopped for friends in high school or grade school for that matter. The world could just as easily have been filled with millions of candidates, girls and boys to potentially become significant people in his life.

In another reality there could have been a host of girls to date, and maybe, just maybe to fall in love with, as if that could ever be such a fate for someone as undesirable as he had come to believe he was.

Sally's voice was suddenly inside his head, there was no external sound. "I think it is a shame that you have become someone you do not want to be. You are an equal to any other creature on your planet. You have everything to offer. It is sad that you have let the world define you instead of you defining the world. You are like a wave crashing on the rocks at the edge of a great ocean. You are as much a part of the ocean as any droplet of water in it. And yet you perceive yourself as being the wave that continues to beat against the unmoving rock, hoping to carve your niche out over the next million years."

Tom looked over at her and said softly, "Who are you and where have you been all of my life?"

"The question really is, where have you been?"

Tom's face reddened slightly, feeling the embarrassment of a life apparently misspent.

"Follow me," he whispered and then set off toward the top of the garage. He had decided to walk the interior, scanning the scene as cars came and went. He began to check the license plates, hoping to spot out of town tourists.

Tom rattled the keys to his own car in his hands, as if to indicate he was looking for his vehicle. Nine cars came and went as they made their way to the top floor. Almost every car had at least one woman or girl on board. Nearly half were mothers taking their young daughters to this shoppers' haven.

"Teach them young," Tom thought and then said, "Are you ok with all of this walking?" They moved into the open air of the uppermost deck. A hint of drizzle quickly turned Tom around.

"I am enjoying my time with you, Tom."

He paused to consider the strangeness of the creature by his side, her lips never parting as she spoke clearly and directly to him. He again began to wonder if she was making any true sound at all or if it was all in his head.

"Come on," he said and headed back down the sloping passage to the fourth level.

Three cars parked, all with local plates. Tom was beginning to feel like he was casing a bank before a robbery. The flow of vehicles was slow but steady.

On the third floor a black sedan pulled into an empty space. The license plate was from Florida. A dark haired Hispanic woman exited the car on the driver's side. Two young women got out on the right side of the car, front and back. Both appeared to be in their late twenties or early thirties. The woman exiting the back seat leaned back in and retrieved an infant child.

Tom was transfixed, almost stopping to stare at the group. Realizing his suspect actions, he sought to minimize the exposure by crossing to the other side of the garage floor. The trio talked amicably amongst themselves, sometimes speaking in English and occasionally reverting to Spanish, especially the mother.

All three of the women were alluring. Tom tried not to look directly at them as they made their way to the stairs. Tom stopped, as if making a decision, allowing them to enter the closed stairwell and then resumed his pace. He and Soli followed them down to the street level and across to the front entrance of the mall itself. The observing pair stayed back, a good thirty or forty feet behind the shoppers. Tom pretended to engage in a conversation with Soli.

He randomly talked about the weather and his boring work day as they entered the massive building, finding themselves in one of the cornerstone department stores. The younger siblings were laughing now, making their way through the store and into the greater hall beyond.

"You are interested?" Sally's voice in his head startled him. He nodded, not quite sure himself. As he looked around he saw a dozen other young women, around the same age or a bit older. Several were attractive. A blond and two brunettes eyed the pair as they passed, as much people watching as they were.

"The younger one without the baby, I think," Tom whispered into Soli's ear. She nodded and then proceeded to speed up her pace to draw closer to the family. Tom increased his pace to keep up. A cluster of college girls, some sporting Green Wave t-shirts, giggled and chatted loudly as they came out of a cosmetics shop.

The Floridians continued until they came to the foot of an escalator leading up to the second floor. It included a food court, a few shops, and an indoor theater at the far end. Tom could make out their conversation as they drew ever closer. They were intent on catching a movie but would get something to eat first. The single daughter opted to use the restroom and broke off from the others. Sally left Tom's side and followed her into the ladies' lavatory. Heart pounding at this sudden turn of events, Tom decided to loiter outside the restroom's entrance, waiting for his "girlfriend's" return.

Five minutes later the young Hispanic woman came out of the restroom, eyeing Tom without any apparent suspicion as she made her way toward the food court. In fact, she had smiled as their eyes made contact and he had happily smiled back.

Tom waited for Soli to exit. Another five minutes went by, then ten.

Suddenly, a female voice from behind, "Is that you Tom?" Tom whirled around, trying not to act too startled. He found himself facing Nancy Baker and another young lady he did not recognize. Nancy was looking him over.

"Didn't think you were much of a sports fan back in your high school days," she said, eyeing the cap. "More of a geek," she turned to giggle at her companion. "My friend Sally Parker had eyes for him back in high school," she continued talking now as if Tom was not there. "Wound up with him anyhow, for whatever reasons." She made this statement as if still trying to sort out her friend's obvious misjudgment in men. Then, "Where's Sally?"

"I came over to see a movie that was no longer playing locally. Sally wasn't interested." He prayed that Sally Number Two would not suddenly appear. "What a disaster," he thought. "Soli, if you can hear me, stay away from me until these assholes leave!"

Nancy smirked, "If I didn't know any better I'd say you were out Tom-catting around." She laughed at her own little joke and her friend echoed the derisive mirth. "See ya," she said dismissively and the pair headed for the theater ticket booth.

Seething, Tom hissed quietly, "Soli, where are you?" No response.

Hesitantly Tom decided to head for the food court. Maybe he missed Soli and she was there observing. The family was sharing pizza and salads. The infant was gurgling with pleasure gnawing on the edge of a pizza slice offered by her grandmother.

Tom ordered a coke at a nearby sandwich shop and found his way to a table close enough to eavesdrop. Soli was nowhere to be seen. Then he caught wind of the current conversation three tables down.

"It is going to be lonely again without my little sister around," said the infant's mother.

"Sí mi hija dulce, te extrañaremos mucho," The older woman reiterated.

"Loyola is such a long way from home. But we will come visit as often as we can and you must be home for Christmas," her sister insisted.

As the conversation continued, Tom was beginning to get the gist of their current circumstances. The group had stopped at the mall after a day of driving the younger daughter, Felicia, back from a three day visit in Tallahassee. The trip had been made to celebrate the birthday of the girl's father. They would be staying in a local Air B n B for the night and then would drop her at the Loyola dorms in the morning before their return trip.

Tom now had to consider the possibility that the duplicate could conceivably run into the original. The odds were against it, but the possibility did exist. His eyes were directed at the far wall but through his peripheral vision he watched the brown-skinned co-ed as she nibbled away at her salad and spoke in the sweetest tones to her supportive family members.

She also interacted with the baby, picking up and rattling a set of large plastic play keys, to get his attention when he began to get fussy. The child responded immediately to her distracting actions and the women continued their conversation until, at last, they had finished, disposed of their plates and utensils and then proceeded to head for the movie theater. The youngster was now over his mother's shoulder and showing signs of sleep. The younger daughter and her mother walked closely together, arms wrapped around each others shoulders.

Tom was smitten. She was about six inches taller than Sally and had an athletic build. She looked like she could have been a competitive swimmer or a runner. She carried herself confidently. Her raven black hair and green tinted eyes beguiled him. If not for Soli, he would have felt her to be way out of his league. He knew sex and fathering babies with this woman would be out of the question, with Soli behind the façade, but her pleasant smile and overall demeanor could surely sustain him for the rest of his life.

Tom liked the idea that she was not just another local girl, like Nancy and her ilk. He realized he wanted something more from life. He knew he could shop forever and possibly come up with someone equal to or greater in looks or presence but he had already made up his mind. She was the one. Now where was Soli?

Just as he was about to get up he saw Felicia heading back toward the eating area. Had she forgotten something? He scanned the floor around their table.

He noted no purses or parcels left unattended. Then she did something quite unexpected, she walked straight over to him and bending down pressed her lips against his cheek.

He stammered, "Hello," not knowing what else to say.

Felicia said, "So nice to finally meet you." Her voice was thick with a soft Spanish accent. She moved over and sat down directly across from him. Then she reached out her hands and took his right hand into hers.

"Soli?" Tom was almost afraid to say the name for fear it would put off this beautiful lady. She nodded affirmatively and squeezed his hand.

"My name is Felicia Soliendo." Soli had to smile appreciatively at the cosmic name connection. I was born in Guatemala but moved to this country with my family ten years ago. We live in Tallahassee, Florida. I had to work hard to save up for my college expenses. I am now twenty-seven years old and in my third year as a graduate student, majoring in Music with a minor in Music Business and Entertainment Industries. I play the piano and enjoy playing volleyball, as well." She paused to let Tom react.

"Wow!" was all he was able to say.

As the two walked back through the mall, Soli explained that she had needed to disappear herself in order to get closer to Felicia. She had been hovering near the Soliendo family as Tom had encountered Nancy and her friend. Even from there she had felt the tension in the disrespectful exchange. She had known, however, that it was best to stay clear and had prudently done so, again focusing on Felicia as Tom bought his Coke and positioned himself nearby.

Once the group had left for their movie, Soli had returned to the restroom, using a stall to cover her transformation into the attractive young Hispanic woman.

Now she and Tom retraced their steps through the mall. Tom had a thought as they made their way through the final department store.

"You are going to need clothes," he said. "Let's go over here and see what we can find."

Tom had always felt that shopping for clothing, or much of anything else for that matter, with Sally, or his mother before that, was an exhaustive and grueling bit of business. However, today was a new day. Today he got to watch as this vision of a girl slowly made her way through rack after rack of clothing. She picked out several dresses, jeans and blouses, and a variety of undergarments with him giving his input during the entire process. Once she had amassed a considerable collection they made their way over to the changing rooms so she could try them on and model for him. He immersed himself in the experience, happily reflecting on his years of thrift and consequential savings. For this occasion, no expense would be spared.

Once the daily ensemble had been sorted out and vigorously approved of, Tom took her over to add some juice to the collection. Now knowing her actual measurements he picked out a dressing gown and a couple of seductive negligees, two pairs of silk stockings and the accoutrements to hold them in place on her shapely body.

Next they were off to the makeup counter, seeking out the basics. Following that, they moved to check out some nearby jewelry, selecting a silver bracelet, a semi-precious stone necklace and matching earrings.

The wait for checkout was now a bit longer than it had been what seemed like just minutes ago. Tom checked his watch. It was nearly nine o' clock and the stores were closing. A steady stream of mall visitors moved towards the outer doors.

154

As Tom handed his bank card to the attendant, he heard a familiar voice, raised just enough for him to hear.

"I knew it! Wait 'til I tell Sally!"

Tom wanted to turn and say something snarky to Nancy but thought better of it. He would have to deal with Sally sooner or later, regardless. Then he realized the real Felicia would be passing their way soon. It was time to go.

As they drove home, Tom wondered what it must be like to encompass someone so intimately, to touch, to feel, to experience every millimeter of that body and then to delve deep into that individual's innermost thoughts, the secrets of another mind.

As Felicia, Soli's demeanor had changed completely. She was quieter, seemingly more introspective. When she spoke the words were intoxicating. And what was most exhilarating about this strange new person was the fact that she acted like they had been friends since childhood. He knew it was Sally's intuitiveness, yet it reflected a complete and total portrayal of this perfect stranger. Sally Number Two was gone. And for the moment, so was Soli.

When they got back to his house it was nearly ten p.m.. The rain had let up but Tom was prudent enough to replace the trusty umbrella in the stand beneath the mailbox for use the next day. As they entered, Rachel ran out. He had forgotten the cat earlier, leaving it in the house after they had left. He shrugged his shoulders unconsciously, realizing that his routine was being picked apart by current events. Nothing lately was routine.

And then he considered work and the coming of tomorrow and the eventual reckoning with Sally. These were things he did not want to think on but knew he must. Felicia had taken a seat on the couch, looking around as if for the first time. Her face was pleasant and she seemed at ease.

"Would you like some strawberry yogurt?" Tom asked as he pulled a small container from the refrigerator.

"Gracious, no." she said demurely.

He got a spoon and then came into the living room to sit next to her on the couch. She smiled as he set down next to her.

"Want to watch some TV?" he invited.

"Why yes, there is a concert on PBS that I heard was going to be aired tonight. It may have started already. Do you mind? Channel 23, mi amor."

Tom turned on the television and punched in the numbers. The wide screen picture materialized on a group of violinists engrossed in Mendelssohn's Violin Concerto in E Minor. It was as if a bright light had switched on in his brain. His world was forever changed. Nothing could ever go back to the way it was. Tom had transformed into a new and different person. He had never been happier. He would, however, have to stop shopping at Walmart.

Sally had heard from her friend Nancy about the sighting at the mall and had protested adamantly via text. After two days of rants and no response from Tom she wrote that she never wanted to see or speak to him again and that he and his slut could go off themselves for all she cared. Tom felt sorry for her, but not that sorry.

Soli had no qualms about being Felicia whenever Tom was at home but during the day she would move about more freely, exploring the neighborhood. Sometimes she would appear to be a stray cat or vaporize completely to get close enough to people to be able watch human behavior or to follow conversations.

As the weeks passed Tom became brave enough to take her out. First they walked three blocks south and made their way up a path to the top of the river levy. Joining a light flow of walkers and bicyclists, they both enjoyed the Mississippi River and the constant parade of ships.

As Tom became more secure, the pair went to museums, then walked through the French Quarter and rode on the streetcars just to get from here to there. Inspired by their previous trip to the mall Tom also decided it was time for him to upgrade his wardrobe. On that excursion she helped him pick out several new shirts, jeans, (which he had seldom worn before), some new slacks, and a new sports jacket.

He actually started getting comments from his co-workers about his new attitude and the unconventional wardrobe changes. He wanted to tell them about his new girlfriend but realized that one day they would want to actually meet her. Despite her outward appearance, she was still an alien being and sooner or later that fact could come to light. It was a chance, unfortunately, that he was not willing to take.

In the mean time, Tom bought Felicia a Yamaha keyboard and a pile of music books. He set her up in the study, dividing the room and making space on the shelves for more of her things. She liked to shop, but she was not impossible about it, often preferring thrift stores for items such as the standing lamp and piano bench she would come to use on a regular basis.

She also got the notion that she wanted to continue her scholastic studies, telling Tom that they would pay for it by setting up a website that would allow her to use her business knowledge to assist fledgling musicians with contract advice and business plans. Everything, of course was in his name, but she would do the lioness's share of the work. He could assist with any bookkeeping issues and build up a potential clientele list for the time when he finally obtained his C.P.A. license. He liked the idea and when he was not studying or she was not playing music or preparing him meals with fresh food as the primary ingredients, she set to work on the project.

On a Saturday afternoon, some weeks later both of them were feeling a bit restless, deciding between them to get out of the house. It was early November and despite the passing of Halloween; the New Orleans days were for the most part balmy and as humid as ever. They had decided to go for a walk in Audubon Park. The temperature was in the upper seventies, perfect for an outdoor excursion.

Parking their car on St. Charles Avenue, the pair wandered into the park, taking the running path toward the river. The ancient oak trees spread over them like a canopy. A shimmer of sunlight reflected off the small silver and green leaves and burnished the Spanish moss that wafted in the light breeze. Eventually they crossed Magazine Street and were making their way behind the Audubon Zoo. They could hear elephants trumpeting in the distance.

In this part of the park there was a great oak tree that had become a landmark in its time. It was the location of a handful of pre-civil war era hangings but had also become the setting for hundreds of weddings in more recent years. The great tree's branches hung low to the ground and offered young people an easy ascent to lookout perches far above the ground.

It was mid-day so the park was quiet and offered an uninterrupted escape for the pair. As if having some adolescent impulse, Felicia led him to the back side of the ancient tree. Behind the massive oak the two were completely hidden from anyone on the not-too-distant one-lane road. No one else was in sight when she pressed him up against the base of the tree, rubbing her soft breasts against his chest.

At first Tom was afraid of getting caught, and then considered the fact that this would only be another frustrated attempt at a sexual encounter. He closed his eyes, thinking, "What the hell."

Even though she could not rub her tongue along them, her lips were full and wet as she pressed them against his. He began to respond, knowing full well the limits of this venture. He was continually amazed by the many little ways that she had sought to convey her love to him.

He began groping her now, his hands finding her ample breasts, feeling the hardening nipples beneath the silky cloth of her low-cut camisole blouse and partially revealed push up bra.

He whispered in her ear, "I could eat you alive." And proceeded to kiss her gently, moving lower onto her neck and then the crowns of her swelling breasts.

As if a switch had been flipped, Felicia was now standing in her bare feet with nothing on but a lacy black bra and a matching pair of black panties. She had not retreated from him but continued to press into him, desiring more of his affection as he reached up to pull the bra down below her nipples. Without hesitating he sucked on each one intently, no longer caring about anyone interrupting the sensuous episode.

Now his hands were on the voluptuous cheeks of her buttocks, cupping and rubbing them as he continued to lose himself in her now heaving breasts.

Suddenly he felt the wetness of a passing shower, reluctantly looking skyward to see a low cloud hovering over the park. He had not thought to bring the umbrella and at this particular moment in time he did not want to be distracted by the insistent dripping that now was beginning to soak his uncovered hair. The rain intensified, as did their passion under the great tree.

He heard a gentle voice in his head, "Let it be Tom, let it be our connection."

Tom had no chance to ask her what she meant. Another switch had flipped and the beautiful Hispanic woman was naked. Her hands reached for his belt. He started to protest, putting his hands on hers, then relaxed and let her continue.

Felicia unfastened the belt, unbuttoned the button beneath it, unzipped the new jeans he was wearing, and tugged them down to his ankles. Water continued to fall from the sky as she pulled his manhood out of his boxers. The rain began to pour down with force. It was drenching his skin and clothing but he was lost in her eyes. Another switch was thrown and Felicia vanished in front of his eyes.

A shot of panic ran through him as he turned his head side to side in search of her. He reached down to redress himself but felt something in his way. Her body was still pressed up against his. She had become liquid, transparent. He felt her fluid hands stroking him until he was hard, then she placed him into the hidden cavity of her liquid body. Her splashing hips thrust up against his pelvis, and he found himself thrusting back. He put his hands on the tree behind him for support, feeling wave after wave of a familiar sensation. It felt just like a woman's orgasm. He exploded into her.

"Oh Soli!" he cried out as he felt himself pull out of her. In front of him was a fully-clothed Felicia. She had a broad smile on her face and helped him redress. He was fighting to remain standing, a weakness in his legs causing them to tremble.

"Esta bien, mi amor?" she said as the rain dissipated with the passing of the clouds above. He grabbed her and hugged her tightly.

"I love you," he said breathlessly and she knew he meant it.

"It is time for me to go now," she said and smiled.

"Ok, we should get home and change out of these wet clothes anyway." He turned to take the first step back toward the distant waiting car.

"No, Tom, I must go now." She stared into his eyes intently. "I will never forget you, or the time we have spent together."

"What?"

The words felt like a kick in the gut. She sensed his discomfort and pulled him close again, hugging him tenderly. Her touch instantly melted all of his anxiety.

"You and I will always be connected. Our waves will cross many times as we move through time. You may not understand this now but when you are ready to become one with everything that is, you will find me and I will find you." She saw the confusion in his eyes, felt the struggle to understand within the beating of his heart.

"As you have chosen this form you have dedicated yourself to your own reality. I think, for many of your years you have lost sight of who you really are, who you are truly destined to become."

"I am yours, Soli," Tom protested.

"No one can truly keep another, Tom. We are not meant to be possessions. Every wave is traveling at its own time and speed. Everything we create along the way is only a product of our own consciousness. You believe your life would be made better, spent with someone like Felicia. Go and find her. You are worthy of any woman you choose. You are only as weak or wanting as you give yourself to believe. Do not let other voices tell you anything different. Separate yourself from the negative.

160

Amplify the positive. Let joy fill your being. Let love rule your universe! I will be with you always."

And with that she was gone. With tears in his eyes Tom thought he saw a small blue orb floating up beyond the canopy of oaks. He rubbed his eyes and then there was nothing.

Back at the house Tom found Rachel preening herself on the couch. He shook his head and then said, "It's you and me Rachel, now and forever."

The black cat purred in response. Disregarding his soaked clothes Tom now wandered into his study. On his desk he discovered a computer print out note. It read:

My dearest Tom,

When I explored Felicia I also checked out the contents of her purse. Below is her phone number and address at Loyola. I also took note of a flyer that she was carrying. It said she will be playing tomorrow night at Snug Harbor. I think you will enjoy the vibrations. Good luck, my love.

Always and Forever,
Soli.